THE BIG CATCH

Was that a ripple? I sit up. Yes! The bobber on my line is moving. I twitch the pole slightly to get the fish to bite. That's called setting the hook. A second later, the red ball goes under the water then pops back up. I've got something, all right! I get a firm grip on my pole with my left hand and start winding the reel with my right.

Joe's ears go up.

Will stops hoovering marshmallows. He shoves Doyle. "Scab's got a bite."

Doyle opens his eyes. I am winding the reel like a madman. At last, the lead sinker breaks the surface. I see the top of the hook, my sister's dragonfly barrette, a marshmallow, a slice of hot dog, a wiggly piece of shrimp . . . and . . . the sun is blinding . . . I've got . . .

I've got . . .

SECRETS OF A LAB RAT

no girls allowed (dogs okay)

mom, there's a dinosaur in beeson's lake

scab for ~~president~~ vice-~~president~~
~~secretary~~ treasurer?

TRUDI TRUEIT

SeCReTS of a LaB RaT

MOM, THERE'S A DINOSAUR IN BEESON'S LAKE

ILLUSTRATED BY **JIM PAILLOT**

ALADDIN

new york   london   toronto   sydney

ALADDIN

An imprint of Simon & Schuster Children's Publishing Division

1230 Avenue of the Americas, New York, NY 10020

First Aladdin paperback edition March 2011

Text copyright © 2010 by Trudi Trueit

Illustrations copyright © 2010 by Jim Paillot

All rights reserved, including the right of reproduction in whole or in part in any form.

ALADDIN is a trademark of Simon & Schuster, Inc.,

and related logo is a registered trademark of Simon & Schuster, Inc.

Also available in an Aladdin hardcover edition.

For information about special discounts for bulk purchases,

please contact Simon & Schuster Special Sales at 1-866-506-1949

or business@simonandschuster.com.

The Simon & Schuster Speakers Bureau can bring authors to your live event.

For more information or to book an event contact the Simon & Schuster Speakers

Bureau at 1-866-248-3049 or visit our website at www.simonspeakers.com.

Designed by Karin Paprocki

The text of this book was set in Minister Light.

The illustrations for this book were rendered digitally.

Manufactured in the United States of America 0611 OFF

2 4 6 8 10 9 7 5 3

ISBN 978-1-4169-6112-3 (pbk)

ISBN 978-1-4169-7593-9 (hc)

ISBN 978-1-4169-9877-8 (eBook)

For Bailey,

and curious scientists everywhere

✶ ACKNOWLEDGMENTS ✶

I am fortunate to have more than a few extraordinary women in my life that make a profound impact on who I am and what I do. My mother, Shirley; my sister, Lori Dru; and my sisters-in-law, Jennifer and Tammy, inspire me to be my best self. Hope, Joy, Esther, Debbie, and Marie remind me to take time to laugh and love. Gail, Connie, Kay, Angela, Tonya, Lisa, Julie, and Debbie N. remain steadfastly with me on the journey, even when the road gets a bit rough. Liesa Abrams, my incredibly talented editor and friend, lights my path with her passion for all things literary. Rosemary Stimola, my ever patient agent and friend, knows just what to say and just when to say it. And Trina, my niece, is the keeper of my heart, now and forever.

MOM, THERE'S A
DINOSAUR IN
BEESON'S LAKE

Big Trouble at Little Creek

veryone's already in the water, Scab." My mom is standing outside the boys' locker room at the Little Creek Swim Club. I am standing in it. "Scab? Are you in there?"

"No."

Oops.

"Your class is starting."

"I don't care."

"You'll care plenty when you're stuck on land this summer."

Bug spit! Why did I make that dumb promise? I hate swimming. And I really hate swimming lessons. So why did I promise to take another session if my parents would let me go sturgeon fishing with Uncle Ant? Easy. I'd have said *anything* to get them to say yes to the fishing trip.

"You don't want to fall off your uncle's boat and drown because you didn't practice treading," my mother calls. Her voice ping-pongs off the tiles. "You don't want to drown, do you?"

I take a long look at myself in the mirror.

"Scab?"

"I'm thinking it over."

"I'm sure it isn't that bad, Squiggle Bear."

I shiver. And not just because she called me that nickname loud enough for the whole pool to hear. "I look stupid, Mom."

"If you would have come to the mall with Isabelle and me . . ."

Shopping with my mother and twin sister is *the* worst torture ever. This is how it works: Isabelle takes a bunch of clothes into the dressing room. After a while, she runs out crying, "Everything is so ugly." That's when I say, "Maybe it's not the clothes," and get nailed with a hanger. Why do girls get so pruny over clothes anyway? I don't care what I wear. As long as it's dark blue. Dark blue trash bag? Okay by me.

"Do they fit, Scab?"

"Yeah, but—"

"Then come *on*. We'll work it out later."

Doesn't she get it? Look at me. Just *look* at me! No, don't. It's too embarrassing. Let me wrap up in my dark blue beach towel. Okay, now you can look. I know, I've got skinny arms, but they can move fast if Lewis Pigford even thinks about

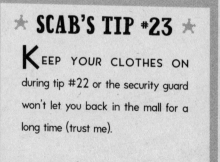

★ **SCAB'S TIP #22** ★

WHILE WAITING FOR YOUR mom to shop, take all the clothes off the dummies. Pose the dummies so they are saluting the people that come off the escalator. Score bonus points: Stand next to the naked dummies and salute, too, while humming "The Battle Hymn of the Republic."

★ **SCAB'S TIP #23** ★

KEEP YOUR CLOTHES ON during tip #22 or the security guard won't let you back in the mall for a long time (trust me).

snagging my double-fudge brownie at lunch. My legs are covered in bruises and scrapes from my daredevil stunts. See that patch of skin missing from my left knee? I did that on the Mighty Maze, the obstacle course that Doyle, Will Greenleaf, and I set up in my backyard.

I was a human rocket. After blastoff I zigzagged

through six stacks of paint cans, snake-slithered on my belly under the big tarp, and flew across the croc-infested water trap without so much as dipping a toe into water (okay, there weren't really any crocs in the kiddie pool). Once I scrambled over Joe's doghouse, however, I ran into trouble—namely Joe. My yellow Labrador grabbed my foot. As usual, Joe wanted to

tarp

mom's heRB
gaRden

CRocodiLe
WateR
tRaP

RoseBushes

play. I wanted to finish. I did better on my second try. I set a new world-record time of 22.5 seconds. I am the Mighty Maze king! But that was yesterday. Nineteen and a half hours ago. Forever ago.

My best friend, Doyle Ferguson, peers around the corner into the locker room. He's dripping wet. "You comin' out this century, Scab, or not?" He's talking loudly, which means my mother sent him in here after me.

I hold my towel tighter. "Not."

"Cool by me," he says in a normal voice. He yanks on the string of his black swim trunks. Plain, black trunks. Lucky guy.

"Give me a sec to make it look like I tried to talk you out," says Doyle. "Then I'll tell Ashlynn."

"Who?"

"Our swim teacher. She's in high school." He grins. "*High* school."

It's going to take a lot more than a cute older girl to get me out there.

"I'll tell Ashlynn you're afraid of the water—"

"Am not," I say. "I can swim better than anybody out there."

"Even me?"

"Even you." And he knows it too.

"Even your sister?" We both know nobody does anything better than Isabelle.

I puff out my chest. "Especially her."

"Prove it."

I watch myself deflate. "I'd . . . uh . . . rather not."

"Are you kidding? The guy who flew ten feet, nine inches over Alec's Super Colossal Dirt Bike Ramp, the guy who burned through the Mighty Maze in twenty-three seconds, the guy who ate a wad of *dryer lint*—"

TOP SECRET!
★ SCAB'S PERSONAL 411 ★

Enter Password: _____ ACCESS DENIED

Enter Password: _____ ACCESS DENIED

Enter Password: _____ I'll let it go *this* time.

ACCESS GRANTED

★ SCAB'S FEARS ★

FEAR	WHY?
Deep water	I can't touch bottom!
Enchiladas	I don't trust food that's folded. (Who knows what it's hiding?)
Automatic sliding doors	Squish-o-matic your kid at the Food Mart! Have a nice day. ☺
The letter G	I can't write it in cursive. My teacher, Miss Sweetandsour, says my G's are saggy. So are her ears.
Ferns	Freaky branches? Curly tendrils? Spores?? Hello, alien species!
Getting lost	I'd miss my dog, Joe; my friends; and my family (even Tattletale Isabelle).

"Twenty-two and a half seconds," I correct. "And I'm telling you, I can't go out there."

"Why not?"

"Because."

"Because *why*? Are you a fraidy cat?"

"No." I am starting to feeling warm.

"Then why? Meow, meow—"

"Just because." I grit my teeth.

"Meow. Me-oooooow." He sounds like Will's cat, Mayonnaise, before they got him fixed. The cat, I mean. Not Will. Doyle holds his arms up and lets his wrists go limp like paws. He claws the air. "Meow, meow. Why, Scab?"

"Because—"

"*Why*? Meee—"

"Because *THIS*!" I let go of the towel.

"—yooow." Doyle's jaw drops.

He cannot believe it. He wipes his eyes, but we both know there is nothing wrong with his vision. It is me. It is all me. I am wearing school-bus yellow swim trunks covered in—I can hardly say it—squirrels.

From my stomach to my knees there's nothing but squirrels: big squirrels and little squirrels, gray squirrels and red squirrels, fat squirrels and skinny squirrels, boy squirrels and girl squirrels. Each squirrel has a fluffy tail. Each squirrel is holding a big acorn. It gets worse. Much worse.

Doyle lowers his fake paws. "Are they—?"

"Yeah." I moan. "They're dancing."

Some of the squirrels are wearing tuxedos and tap dancing. Others are swaying in hula skirts. A few aren't wearing anything.

I know my sister was involved in this. She probably told my mother squirrels were the newest thing in swim trunks. And by now, Tattletale Isabelle has probably gossiped to everyone out there, including Ashlynn, that I am wearing this ridiculous suit. My class is waiting for me to come out so they can laugh it up. But I'm not going out. No way. No how. No chance.

"Doyle? Scab? What's going on in there?"

"Your mom," croaks Doyle.

"Boys, let's go!"

"What do we do?"

Our heads swivel between the front door and the pool entrance. The front door. The pool entrance. The front—

"Salvatore Wallingford McNally! Are you coming out or do I have to come in?"

"NO!"

That's all I need: for every kid at River Rock Elementary to know that my mother marched into the boys' locker room at the Little Creek Swim Club and hauled me out to the pool by the seat of my squirrel-print swim trunks.

"I'm coming out!" I cry.

Doyle gasps.

"If I want to go fishing with Uncle Ant, I've got no other choice," I remind him. I take a deep breath. "This is for the fish."

"For the fish," he says.

We knock knuckles.

Doyle slaps me on the back. "You're the bravest kid in the universe, Scab."

I nod, though I know it isn't true. If I'm lucky, Doyle will never know how close he came to guessing the truth: that I am a fraidy cat, after all.

I clench my teeth. I clench my fists. I clench my dancing-squirrel butt.

And I take the longest walk of my short life.

Warning: Squirrel Crossing

oyle and I rush past a sign that says no running as fast as we can without running. He waves to a dark-haired older girl standing in the shallow end of the pool. That must be Ashlynn.

I don't wave. I have a plan. My beach towel is wrapped around my waist so tightly it's digging into my skin. Our class is in the water. They are lined up along the edge of the pool, practicing the scissors kick. Seven pairs of eyes, including my sister's, follow us. I fling off my towel, squat, and hop in the water. Ha! Two seconds tops. Nobody could have possibly seen—

"Nice squirrels, McNally," hoots Lewis Pigford.

Everyone snickers. Except my sister. She looks away. I knew it! Isabelle tattled. My twin is forever telling people about the stuff I do, the stuff I don't do, and the stuff she thinks I should do.

We just turned ten years old, but I am in the fourth grade and she is in the fifth. Isabelle got moved ahead this year because she is smart times ten. I wish Isabelle would get moved ahead in swim class too. That way, I wouldn't have to worry about her reporting back to our parents every single thing I do, don't do, or should do in the water.

★ SCAB'S POOL-TIME FUN ★

★ Have a contest to see who can make the biggest fart bubble in the pool (hint: eat a bowl of superspicy chili four hours before you go swimming and you'll win every time).

★ Tell your sister you threw a quarter in the pool. Tell her if she finds it, she can keep it. A half hour later, when she says she has searched every inch of the pool and can't find the quarter, gasp and say, "Quarter? Did I say 'quarter'? I meant 'rock.'"

★ During the lap swim time, swim in circles. When the lifeguard shouts at you to do laps like everyone else, yell back that you can't swim in a straight line because one arm is shorter than the other.

★ Did you know the human body is made up of 80 percent water? While in the pool, go up to a second grader and tell him this fact, then clutch your stomach and scream, "Go get help! I'm leaking!"

"This pool is freezing," says Doyle as we kick. His lips are turning blue.

"I don't think so," I say. "If it were freezing, the temperature would be thirty-two degrees Fahrenheit. Then it wouldn't be water anymore. It would be ice."

"Thanks, Science Boy."

"You're welcome."

Ashlynn is beside me. "Are you Salvatore—"

"Scab. Everybody calls me Scab."

"'Cause it's better than Sally McNally, right, Scab?" yells Lewis.

Everyone giggles.

Most people ask how I got my nickname. I have to explain about the time I went to summer camp and got 148 itchy, oozy, swollen, red mosquito bites. That's when Doyle started calling me Scab. It stuck. The name, I mean, not the scabs. I peeled off all the scabs. Wouldn't you?

But Ashlynn doesn't ask about my name. Instead she says, "Point your toes when you kick, okay? That's it. You've got it, Scab." She moves on to help Cloey Zittle. "Easy, Cloey. You're not trying to escape Jaws . . ."

I am in the intermediate swim class. We're called the Salmon. You think *that's* a stupid name? Last year I was a Guppy. The littlest kids are Tadpoles, then come Guppies, Salmon, Dolphins, and Orcas. I wonder what's after that—the Giant Man-Eating Squids?

Thweeeeeeet.

Ashlynn just blew her whistle. "Crawl-stroke across the shallow end," she shouts. After we swim two laps, we practice floating. This is all stuff I did last year, so it should be easy. At first I forget to arch my back so I get water up my nose and in my mouth. I don't swallow, because I *know* what Lewis does in the water.

"Look, Doyle," I call, spitting water high into the air. "I'm a fountain."

He laughs.

"That's it for today," calls Ashlynn. "Great job, Salmon. On Tuesday we'll start learning the breast-stroke—"

Lewis Pigford whistles.

"Oh, grow up, Lewis," snaps Isabelle.

"Anybody who wants to can swim to the deep end and back with me," says Ashlynn. She dives into the water. When her head comes up, she starts doing the crawl stroke.

My sister, Doyle, Cloey, Henry, Beth, Juan, and Emma start racing for the other side of the pool too. I join them because the crawl is my best stroke. When I get to the middle of the pool, where the bottom starts to drop off, I turn back—not because I'm tired.

I have plenty of energy left. It's just that the water is so deep in the Deep End. Too deep. Nobody notices I have gone back, which is good. My towel is still near the edge of the pool. I plan to hop out, wrap it around me, and bolt for the locker room, where I might accidentally forget my squirrel suit after I change, if you know what I mean.

I push myself up over the edge. Water stings my eyes as I reach for my towel. I feel a tug.

"Not so fast." Lewis has got the other end of my towel. "I want to get a good look at those squirrels of yours."

"Let go, Pigford."

"Is that one wearing a tutu?" He loosens his grip. I ease up too, and he whips the towel from me. "Suckerrrrrr!"

"Give it back, Pig—"

"Un-be-lievable." He circles me. I hunch over and try to cover my trunks with my arms, but—dang it—there are just too many squirrels. "Hey, Mapanoo!"

Lewis yells to Henry, but of course everybody looks because they are all swimming this way. "Check out McNally's dancing rodents—"

Suddenly a head pops up out of the water next to us. It's Ashlynn. She flips her dark bangs back with one hand. "Hey, Scab, I almost forgot—"

"Yeah?" I swallow hard. She saw that I didn't swim the length of the pool with the other kids. She

★ AMAZING SQUIRREL TAILS! ★

IF A SQUIRREL FALLS FROM A TREE, IT WILL FIRST use its tail as a parachute to slow itself down, before turning it into a cushion to land on. Flying squirrels rely on their flattened tails to help guide them as they glide through the air. Asia's giant flying squirrel can glide up to 1,500 feet! Squirrels also use their tails to communicate. When a squirrel quickly flips its tail at another squirrel, it means, "Get away, this food is mine!" If only that would work on Lewis! He's always stealing other people's food.

noticed that I only made it halfway. And she is going to ask me why. What do I say? What do I do?

"Great trunks," she says, and disappears under the water.

Lewis throws my towel at my feet. I pick it up and shake it out. Flipping it over my shoulder, I calmly stroll into the locker room. I'm whistlin' all the way.

On the drive home my mother says, "We're going to the mall this weekend, Scab, to pick out some new trunks for you. This time, I don't want any argument—"

"Don't sweat it, Mom," I say. "I'll keep these."

A stunned face looks at me in the rearview mirror. "You'll keep those? But it took you fifteen minutes to come out of the locker room. You said you looked stupid—"

"They're not so bad."

Isabelle snickers. I lightly punch her in the shoulder. She punches back harder.

"'They're not so bad,'" mumbles my mother. "He

couldn't stand them an hour ago, but now he's keeping them." My mother talks to herself when we confuse her. She's been talking to herself *a lot* this year.

"It's all right if I keep them, isn't it?"

"Well, sure. But what on Earth made you change your—"

"Not what," my sister says, jumping in. "Who.

And I know—ewww!" She waves her hand in front of her nose. "Mom! Scab let a toot out the chute! He did it on purpose."

"Salvatore," my mother warns.

"Sorry," I say, but proudly fold my arms and grin.

It's true. I can fart on cue pretty much anywhere, anytime, anyplace. It's my superpower. I am Scab McNally, Fart Boy. I definitely need my own theme song. I'm thinking something with a booming tuba would be nice. You know, a superpower like tooting can really come in handy. Right now Isabelle's got her head out the window, gulping fresh air. She looks like my dog, Joe, except he's got better hair . . . uh, fur. And no fleas. Ha! My sister has forgotten all about telling my mother what Ashlynn said to me. See? Very handy. I'd teach it to you if I could. Honestly, I would. But like I said, it's a gift.

CHAPTER

Reelin' in the Big One

If anybody's interested, I brought tuna on—"

"Sourdough with pickles and olives." Doyle and I finish Will's sentence.

Whenever the three of us go fishing, Will brings tuna salad on sourdough with pickles and olives. His mother has been making that same sandwich for Will as long as I've known him. And for as long as I've known him, Will tries to trade it for something— anything—that isn't tuna salad on sourdough with pickles and olives.

"Anybody want to—"

"No!"

Doyle, who's between Will and me, reels in his line. He checks to see that the earthworm is still on the hook. It is. Doyle casts off again. It's about eight thirty on a Saturday morning. We're the only ones at Beeson's Lake, which is the way we like it. We sit at the end of an old, saggy dock. I don't know who built the dock or when. Or why, really. There are no houses here. No signs pointing the way. You either know how to get to here or you don't. We fish here most every Saturday.

My dog, Joe, lies behind me on the dock. We go everywhere together, except school, of course. He sits in our front window and whimpers when I leave in the morning. The glass is always smudged with his nose prints. Joe hates it when I leave him. I hate it too. I told Doyle I ought to run for class president on

★ JOE AND ME ★

For my tenth birthday, my parents took Isabelle and me to the shelter to pick out a dog. Isabelle wanted a teacup poodle. Upchuck-o-matic. I wanted a Saint Bernard. My mom just wanted out of there. It was a real bark fest! We finally agreed on a yellow Labrador. My sister named him (we had a deal that if she helped me convince my parents to get a dog, she'd get to name it). I was worried because she was leaning toward Precious Puddles. Yech!! Luckily, she chose Joe. It's a long story involving sloppy joes and that onionhead, Lewis Pigford. Joe is supposed to be our dog, but he is really *my* dog. I walk him. I feed him. I scoop up after him. I teach him tricks. He's the best!

Tricks Joe can do:

* Play fetch with my sister's headless Barbie

* Roll over and play dead

* Chase his tail (Is that a trick?)

* Shake hands

* Balance a ball on his nose (almost!)

the promise that I would let kids bring their dogs to school. I bet I would win in a landslide. Or is it "by a landslide"? Either way, I'd win, for sure.

I got Joe for my birthday. He was the best present EVER, even better than the Mount Saint Helen replica volcano I got last year and I *loved* that. I souped up the lava flow engine with extra battery power, maybe

too much battery power. My sister got too close and it spewed a half gallon of orange soda pop all over her. Anyway, Joe is one year, one month, and three days old, which is seven years, seven months, and twenty-one days old in dog time. I think. So far, I've taught him a few tricks, like how to beg, roll over, and chew on Isabelle's shoes instead of mine. I've wanted a dog my whole life. Joe is the greatest dog in the universe. Doyle would probably tease me for saying this, but when I look at Joe I can tell he's wanted a boy his whole life too.

Now and then, Joe's tail flicks against my back.

★ SCAB'S FISH BUFFET BAIT ★

- 1 mini marshmallow
- 1 cheese puff
- 1 piece of lettuce
- 1 slice of uncooked hot dog
- 1 glittery pink dragonfly hair clip (borrowed from your sister)
- 1 shrimp
- 1 worm
- ½ olive

Get the biggest fish hook you can find. Squish everything on the list onto the hook. Cast off and get set to reel in a ton of fish.

I've got his leash on him, because he likes to chase ducks. Once in a while he'll spot one on shore and take off after it. He'll jump right into the lake! It makes my heart take extra beats when he does this, but luckily he never goes far. Ducks can fly. Joe can't. I check again to make sure his leash is wrapped tight around the dock post. It is. I reach over and scratch the top of his neck under his collar—that's his favorite scratching spot, besides his belly. Then I get back to baiting my hook.

"Scab, what are you doing?" Will's got his pole in one hand and a wedge of sandwich in the other. I can smell the stink of tuna all the way over here.

"New invention," Doyle answers first.

"What is it?"

"The perfect bait."

"No such thing."

I lift the hook off my lap. "Until now."

Will laughs. "Geez, Scab, it looks like you're trying for every kind of fish in the lake."

"That's the idea," I say. "Any fish swimming by has got to see *something* here he likes."

"I get it. It's like when my parents take us to the Happy Troll buffet. My mom gets spaghetti, my dad gets steak, and I get pizza."

"You want to donate anything to my Fish Buffet Bait?" I ask.

★ SCAB'S SNOT CAP ★

☑ 1 plastic ring (2 inches in diameter)

☑ 1 baseball cap (make sure you don't need it for Little League)

☑ glue

☑ 1 plastic toilet-paper holder

☑ 1 roll of your favorite toilet tissue

☑ 1 small Nerf ball

Sew the plastic ring on one side of the cap above the ear, near the brim. Glue one end of the plastic toilet-paper holder to the top of the baseball cap (the holder should be sticking straight up). Place a roll of toilet paper on the roller. Cut the Nerf ball in half. Glue half of the Nerf ball on top of the roller to keep the toilet paper secure (keep the other half of the ball as a spare or to make another Snot Cap for a friend). Thread the toilet paper down through the ring so it'll be ready when you feel a sneeze coming on. Wear your Scab's Snot Cap with pride and confidence!

Will plucks an olive from his sandwich and hands it to Doyle, who hands it to me. I am barely able to get the olive onto the end of my bulging hook. "This is the one," I announce. "This is the one that's going to make me famous."

"I sure hope so," says Doyle, giving me a sideways smirk.

I frown. "Just because a couple of my other inventions didn't work out—"

"A couple? You mean, like the licorice toothpaste?"

Will gags. "I had to be the tester on that. Don't forget about the potato-chip seat cushions—you could only use them once."

Doyle nods. "Raincoats for cats."

"Glow-in-the-dark sunglasses," offers Will.

"What was that one with the hat?"

"Hat?"

"You know, with the toilet paper."

Will snaps his fingers. "The Snot Cap—"

"That's it!"

I've heard enough. "When you guys sneeze in front of Ashlynn and there's a giant, green booger swinging from your nose, don't come whining to me," I say.

Doyle snorts. "I'll take a big glob of snot over a roll of toilet paper on my head any day."

"Remember Isabelle's Smell?" asks Will.

"Who could forget Scab's sister-repellant spray?"

"That one worked," I remind them.

"*Too* well," says Will. "We had to evacuate the school. Pee-ewwwww!"

"Quiet. You'll spook the fish."

"What fish?" Doyle scratches a blotchy pink cheek. "Not even the minnows are biting."

"They will now. Here we go, guys." I toss out my line. Unfortunately, the cheese puff and Will's olive fall off my hook while the line is still in midair.

"Don't worry," says Will as we watch the cheese puff sail away. "You've still got plenty of bait left. You'll snag something—"

I nod. "In less than three minutes, I'll bet."

"I'll take that bet," says Will.

Doyle lifts his wrist. "I'll time it." He has the best watch, so he is always our official timer.

Silently, hopefully, we watch my lucky red bobber float on the surface. Doyle watches his watch *and* my bobber. Will shifts. Doyle sneezes. I shift. Doyle sneezes again. My dog yawns.

"How long has it been?" I whisper after what I am sure is three minutes.

"A minute, twelve," says Doyle.

Three minutes comes and goes—nothing. Ten—still nothing. By twenty, Doyle and Joe are stretched out on the dock. Will's got his head in my bag of mini marshmallows. I am eating the other half of his tuna on sourdough with pickles and olives, while counting lily pads. One hundred twenty-seven, one hundred twenty-eight, one hundred twenty-nine . . .

Was that a ripple? I sit up. Yes! The bobber on my line is moving. I twitch the pole slightly to get the fish to bite. That's called setting the hook. A second later, the red ball goes under the water then pops back up. I've got something, all right! I get a firm grip on my pole with my left hand and start winding the reel with my right.

Joe's ears go up.

Will stops hoovering marshmallows. He shoves Doyle. "Scab's got a bite."

Doyle opens his eyes. I am winding the reel like a madman. At last, the lead sinker breaks the surface. I see the top of the hook, my sister's dragonfly barrette, a marshmallow, a slice of hot dog, a wiggly piece of shrimp . . . and . . . the sun is blinding . . . I've got . . .

I've got . . .

Boy Overboard!

n empty hook.

Bug spit!

"Tough break," says Doyle.

"Good try," says Will.

Joe lets out a tiny wail. He puts his head back down like he's embarrassed to be my dog.

I know I had something. I *know* it. What could have happened? A few seconds later I get my answer. The water near where my line went in starts to bubble, then a pond turtle pulls itself up onto a lily pad. Double bug spit!

Will says what we already know. "Turtle must have gone for your lettuce."

★ 37 ★

★ SCAB'S TIP #37 ★

To keep bugs from biting you, rub a dryer sheet on your arms and legs before you go outside (it would have helped to know this before I went to summer camp and got eaten alive). If your mom is out of dryer sheets, do not substitute them with slices of American cheese. This turns you into a human hamburger and triples your insect bites.

I slap away an enormous mosquito that's feasting on my arm.

An hour later, Will has eaten all my cheese puffs. There's a huge red welt on my arm where the mutant mosquito tried to suck me dry. And we haven't caught a thing.

"I gotta get going," says Will, licking his orange fingers.

"Me too," says Doyle. His cheeks are lobster red.

I am not ready to give up. "How about another half hour to see if my perfect bait—"

"No such thing," says Will.

The guys start packing up. I slump down. Maybe he's right. So far, my Fish Buffet Bait is a disaster. The score is turtles: 1, Scab: nothing. I open my tackle box.

"Worms are the best bait," says Will.

"Everything likes worms," says Doyle. "And when you think about it, worms like everything."

"Like what?" asks Will.

"Dead bodies, for one," Doyle says. His mom runs the Peaceful Meadows Funeral Home, so he ought to know.

My head snaps up. Was that something? Did the bobber on my line wiggle? Whoa! There it is again. I set the hook. Come on, perfect fish bait! *Come oooooon!* I have something to prove here.

Doyle is still talking. ". . . worms eat everything and anything, you know—skin, guts, hair—everything except bone."

Ah, the tug. This is it! Gently, gently, gently I start reeling in my line. Right away I know I've got something because I can feel the tension this time. And this fella is no squatty minnow, that's for sure. "Guys," I whisper. "I've got—"

"Eyeballs are their favorites," Doyle informs Will.

"How do you know?"

"I know."

"What about the casket? Doesn't that stop 'em from chewing on the dead guy?"

"You can buy one of the fancy metal ones, but they'll still find a way to get in. Face it, Will, after you croak you're going to get munched on by gobs of gooey earthworms."

"Cool."

My pole is arcing like a rainbow. It's getting tougher

to crank the reel. Blue veins are popping up on my forearms. This fish is *huge*. I grit my teeth. *"Guys?"*

"E-roo?" squeaks Joe, lifting an ear. At least somebody's paying attention.

"My cousin Norwood has a tapeworm," says Will, shutting his tackle box. "He ate raw meat or something."

"Now *that* is cool," says Doyle. "Is the worm eating his eyeballs from the inside out?"

"I don't know. I'll ask."

My rod is about to break. So are my arms. My feet are skidding toward the edge of the dock. Dribbles of sweat are falling into my eyes. "GUYS!"

They turn. *"What?"*

Doyle's lobster face goes chalk white. Will drops his tin of bobbers.

"Scab!"

"Hold on! We're coming."

Joe trots back and forth behind me. "Ow-ooooo!"

Now he's going to do the Lassie warning howl. Great timing. Thanks, boy.

My strength is going, along with most of the rubber on the bottom of my tennis shoes. I make up my mind. No matter what happens I can't let go. I *won't* let go. I see my reflection in the black water. It's coming up to meet me. "Yeeeeee-ahhhhhhhhhh!" I scream. My arms are being ripped from their sockets. This is it. I can't hang on anymore. I'm going in!

I shut my eyes, clamp my jaw, and wait for the cold and wet to smack me. I wait . . .

★ SCAB'S FISHING JOURNAL ★

March 29—I caught my first fish this year! Sweet! It was a sunfish, about four inches long, a quarter pound. I think. Unfortunately, I also lost my first fish this year when it slipped through my fingers and back into the lake. Note: Never eat barbecue potato chips while fishing!

April 5—Doyle caught a three-inch minnow. Will caught a six-inch brook trout. I caught a nine-day cold.

April 12—Same old story. Zip. Nothing. Empty hook-o-rama. Will I *ever* catch anything?

Suddenly, air is whooshing from my lungs. I am flying backward.

Eeeeeeeak! I hear the squeak of soleless tennis shoes against old wood—*my* tennis shoes. The waistband of my jeans is digging into my stomach. It burns. I taste tuna on sourdough with pickles and olives. I swallow hard to keep it down. Will's sandwich is not something you want to taste (or see) twice on the same day. I open my eyes. Doyle is hauling me back by my belt loops. Will's hands are wrapped around mine, steadying my fishing pole. "Reel!" He screams. "Reel, Scab!"

I do what he says.

"Woof!" Joe cheers us on. "Woof, woof, woof!"

"It's enormous!" shouts Doyle. He's got both arms around my waist to anchor me to the dock. "I'll bet it's a channel catfish."

"Or a rainbow trout," hollers Will.

"Could be a kokanee salmon."

"Or a coho."

"Chinook!" they shriek together.

"It's got to be a fifty-pounder."

"No such thing as a fifty-pounder in Beeson's Lake—"

"Until now!" I yell. I am about to catch the biggest fish of the year—maybe of the decade!

"Whatever you do," yells Doyle, "don't let that thing get—"

Crack! My pole breaks. The line snaps. Will and I topple backward. Will nearly goes into the water.

I fall on Doyle. I see a flash of brown. And something else. I think.

"—away," moans Doyle from under my butt.

For a long time we lay sprawled on the dock. Nobody says a word. Joe is licking my face like it's a scoop of double-chunk chocolate fudge ice cream. He does that when he is worried about me.

"We were this close," Doyle finally croaks, sliding out from under me.

"This close," echoes Will.

"We gotta come back here next week—"

"I'm in," says Will.

"How about you, Scab?"

Did someone say something?

"Scab? Are you hurt?"

"No." I pat Joe's head. "I'm all right, boy." He stops licking but doesn't move an inch. "I'm all right," I say again.

"You did it, buddy." Doyle pounds my knee with his fist. "You made the perfect bait."

Clutching what's left of my pole, I stare into the choppy water.

"We'll catch him next time. We'll all bait our hooks exactly the way you did today and we'll get that big boy—"

"With my olives? You want to use my olives, too?"

"That's what 'exactly' means, Will."

"I'll bring tuna on sourdough with pickles and olives for everybody."

"If you have to," groans Doyle. He picks up his gear and heads down the dock.

Will follows him. "But you said . . ."

My pole is toast. The top third is gone. The crank is bent. My uncle Ant gave me this pole for my birthday last year, and I'm sure sad to lose it. But that's not what's bothering me. Not really. I've been fishing with my dad and uncle since I was four years old. I've seen just about every kind of fish there is. I've seen fish with ridges and spines and bulges and feelers, but I've *never* seen a fish like this. I have never in my life seen a fish with a . . . a . . . a neck!

That's what I saw, all right—a long, chocolate brown, leathery neck.

Maybe.

I kneel down and whisper into Joe's ear, "What do you think?"

Joe tips his head, thumping his tail against my knee.

"I'm not sure either," I say.

"Scab?" Doyle is calling from the shore. "You coming?"

"Yep. Come on, Joe." Tucking what's left of my pole under my arm, I grab Joe's leash and my tackle box. We head down the dock. Before I step onto the dirt, I glance back.

I see clumps of grasses and cattails.

I see blankets of lily pads.

I see one tippy dock leading to the calmest, blackest waters on Earth. And that's all I see. Good.

Good.

The Password Is: "Doomed"

cab!" My doorknob rattles. "I want to talk to you!"

More rattling.

Joe's head pops out of a stack of my clothes—pile number three, to be exact. He's got one of my socks in his mouth. I think it's a clean sock. Hard to say. I forget which piles are clean and which ones are dirty.

"Don't worry, it's double locked. Isabelle can't get in."

Joe cocks an ear. He dives back into the clothes until all that's visible is one golden flag of a tail waving back and forth. I laugh.

I'm mashing unsalted sunflower seeds, unsalted peanuts, and cereal bran flakes to make Scab's Trail Mix for Hamsters. It's for Will's red teddy bear hamster, Donald Trump. Actually, Donald is a girl. We didn't know he was a she until he/she had six babies with Jay Leno—that's Will's blue hamster. We *were* going to change her name to something girly, but after Donald ate two of her babies, we figured it was okay to let it slide.

I was pretty excited when Will told me that

★ RODENTS ON THE GO ★

Hamsters are nocturnal, which means they like to sleep during the day and stay up at night. They have tons of energy and can run up to five miles a night! No wonder Will has a big hamster wheel. I wonder if he'll let me put an odometer on that thing! Hamsters have sharp front teeth for gnawing. Their teeth keep growing throughout their whole lives. Did you know girl hamsters can have up to eighteen babies in one litter? Once, a hamster had twenty-six babies! That's a lot of kids to name.

SCAB'S NEED-TO-KNOW
★ GERMAN PHRASES ★

Guten Morgen.	Good morning.
Ich heisse _____.	My name is _____.
Ich muss jetzt pinkeln!	I have to whiz now!
Mach die Tür auf, Eidechsenlippen.	Open the door, Lizard Lips.
Meine Schwester ist ein Hamsterkopf.	My sister is a hamster head.

*Did you know "hamster" is a German word that means "to forage and hoard"? My sister hoards peanut butter cookies. She hides them in the head of her Hairdo Heidi. Heidi doesn't have a body. She's just a giant head full of cookies. Let me know when you're hungry and we'll pop her skull.

Donald and Jay had babies, because you figure a red hamster and a blue hamster are going to have purple kids, right? Wrong. Turns out "red" really means light orange and "blue" means gray. Bummer. I throw a handful of dried peas in the bowl. Then I take some out because I remember Will said too many vegetables can give hamsters the runs.

Speaking of the runs, Isabelle is still outside my lab. She is pounding on the door. "*Mach die Tür auf, Eidechsenlippen.*" My sister likes to show how smart she is by using big words. Or German words. Or big, German words. Ignore her. I do.

"Scab, I'm telling Mom."

"What's the password?" I tease.

"Dragonfly."

I stop mashing. I open the door to find one scowling sister with her hands on her hips. "Better watch it, Izzy, or your face is going to freeze like— oops, too late."

She sticks her palm out. "Hand it over."

I pull on my front belt loop. "What?"

"You know what."

"I don't know what." I hop from one foot to the other. "And who says I have it even if I did know what?"

"Don't you?"

"No." I can say this easily because I don't have her barrette. Anymore.

"What about Joe?"

At the sound of his name, my dog's head pops out the side of pile number three. He's got a pair of my underwear on his face. His nose is sticking out of a leg hole.

"Look at him," she accuses. "He chews up everything. I don't know how many times I've caught him ripping my shoes to shreds."

I bite my lip.

Isabelle starts for my dog. "I bet Joe took my—"

I jump in front of the pile and put up both hands. It's one thing to mess with me. It's another to mess with my dog. "He didn't."

She frowns. "How do you know?"

"He likes to chew on soft stuff, like socks and slippers, not barrettes. Joe wouldn't take it. He didn't take it," I say firmly. I feel like a lawyer.

"Ruff," says my client.

"I guess you're right." Isabelle turns away. She rubs her forehead. "It's just so strange. I always keep it in the top drawer of my dresser between my butterfly clip and ladybug headband. What could have happened to it?"

I shrug, and start strumming my teeth with my fingernail.

"If I lost it at school, I'll never find it. . . . I bet that new girl, Gwyneth, took it—she's always taking things out of my desk without asking. . . ." Her voice breaks. Her shoulders shake. "I really loved that dragonfly barrette. Great-Aunt Sarah gave it to me, you know, before she died."

Ah, geeeeez. Is she crying?

Isabelle sniffs. "It was the last Christmas present I ever got from her, and now—"

"Okay, okay," I say. "I took it."

She whirls around. "I knew it."

What an actress! Her cheeks aren't even wet. I should have known. "No fair, Isabelle."

"Yes fair, Scab. I knew you were lying. I can always tell what you're up to because you give it away."

"I do not."

"Want to bet? When you fidget, it means you're lying. When you bob your eyebrows up and down, it means you're up to no good. Let's see, what else? Oh, when your ears turn red, it means you know you're in deep trouble and you're trying to figure out how to get out of it. I know all of your tricks."

MEET MY TWIN SISTER: ★ ISABELLE CATHERINE MCNALLY ★

☑ Description: brown hair, blue eyes, mutant brain, permanent scowl, birthmark on her leg that looks like an accordion (You've got to see it!)

☑ Personality: stubborn, but can be nice when you are sad or sick

☑ Weird talent: instantly knowing when her stuff is missing

☑ Favorite food: frozen cookie dough (She pretends she's going to make cookies for me, but only three cookies ever make it out of the oven.)

☑ Favorite activity: it's a tie between lecturing me about how I'm supposed to behave and tattling to my parents about how I *have* behaved

"I know yours, too. Now bark, roll over, and play dead."

"Woof, woof!" Suddenly, Joe is flying toward me. He rolls onto his back, and sticks his paws in the air.

"Looks like Joe wins the contest." I laugh.

My sister, however, is not laughing. "Hand over my barrette."

I wrap my arms around Joe and sink to the floor. "I . . . uh . . . I can't."

"Why not?"

"I don't . . . exactly . . . um . . . have it."

"What do you mean? Where is it?"

"It's sort of . . . I kind of accidentally . . ."

Her lips disappear. "Where. Is. It."

I lower my head into the safety of Joe's soft neck. "In Beeson's Lake."

"What? I can't hear you."

I look up. "I said, 'In Beeson's Lake.'"

She lets out a shriek. "You threw my dragonfly barrette in the lake?"

"Not on purpose. See, Will, Doyle, and I were fishing, and I was trying out my new Fish Buffet Bait—that's where you put a whole lot of stuff on the hook to get the fish to bite—but I needed something glittery that looked like a bug—"

"You didn't!"

"I was going to bring it back, but the monster grabbed my hook. It took all three of us to hold on to him. We would have caught him, too, if my pole hadn't snapped—"

⁎ SCAB NEWS ⁎
BY ISABELLE C. MCNALLY
(HISTORY CLUB PRESIDENT)

⁎ 8:47 a.m. I caught Scab speed skating on two sheets of paper down the hallway before school. He was racing Doyle. They knocked over the book rack outside the library. Mr. Corbett sent them to the principal's office.

⁎ 8:52 a.m.: That worm Scab wriggled his way out of trouble again. I knew he would!! ☹

⁎ 4:13 p.m.: I discovered my dragonfly barrette was missing. I went to interview the main suspect.

⁎ 4:29 p.m.: Scab confessed to stealing my dragonfly barrette to use as a fishing lure. It's now at the bottom of the lake! Mom, tell him he needs to pay for a new one.

⁎ 4:37 p.m.: Scab threw me out of his lab (how rude!) and locked the door.

⁎ 6:13 p.m.: Weird noises are coming from inside Scab's lab. And it isn't the usual sounds, if you know what I mean.

This concludes Scab News for today. Isabelle Catherine McNally reporting.

P.S. If you want to know why the dryer is making that *kerklunkity-plop* noise, ask Scab about his marble experiment.

"Monster?" She rolls her eyes.

Did I say that?

"I . . . I meant 'fish.' Yeah, yeah, fish. That's what I meant." Will you look at that? My knee *is* twitching. Isabelle may have a point about that lying thing. I clamp my hand over my knee. "It could have been an alligator. Whatever the thing was, it was huge—"

"I want my barrette, Scab."

"But I told you—"

"If it *is* at the bottom of Beeson's Lake, then I guess you'd better pay close attention in swim class tomorrow so you can go get it." She stomps toward the door.

"Swim class?"

"Have you forgotten? We're going to the deep end of the pool to dive."

The Deep End? I jump up. Panic washes over my body. Then I realize Isabelle is teasing me. She has to be. "No, we're not. Ashlynn didn't say anything last week—"

"Did so. She said that after the first class we'd

be working in the middle and deep end for the rest of the session—oh, that's right, you were hiding out in the boys' locker room in your squirrel suit." She giggles. "Well, now you know."

I feel a lump in my throat. Yep. Now I know.

"And you also know I'm *not* kidding. I want my barrette. Or else." My sister stalks out of my room.

Isabelle is kidding. She has to be. I am sure only the older kids, the Dolphins and Orcas, swim in the Deep End.

"Don't you want to know 'or else what'?" Isabelle is back.

"You'll tattle to Mom and Dad in your weekly news report," I say, pushing her out of my lab.

"I'm also going to tell them why the dryer makes that funny noise when you put it on the fluff cycle—"

"Fine. Go write a rough draft." I shut the door behind her. I bolt the lock.

I clear the trail mix off my desk. I have no time for silly stuff like skinny hamsters or lost barrettes or broken clothes dryers. This is serious. I sit down at my desk. Glassy, brown eyes are begging me to play. Joe's got his favorite toy, a squeaky hot dog, in his mouth. "Can't right now, boy," I say, scratching his neck under his collar. "We've got a problem."

Joe drops the toy. He lies down next to my chair. He puts his chin on top of my foot. He likes to do this when I am working on a new invention. I like it too. I put my head down on my desk. What am I going to do? I have less than twenty-four hours to figure out how to keep from going into the Deep End.

Where I can't touch bottom.

One Toe-riffic Class

"Ick!" Cloey Zittle is standing by the shallow end of the pool. "Scab, what happened to your foot?"

"Motorcycle accident." I hobble toward her. "I did a wheelie on Hangman's Bridge."

"Ohmigosh, really?"

"I sliced through my big toe. See where it's kind of green? They had to sew that part back on—"

Cloey's orange flip-flops make a sharp U-turn on the concrete. "Mooooooom."

I hide my grin. This is going to be easier than I thought. My dad dropped us off today and my mom is picking us up after class so there are no parents to worry about. However, Tattletale Isabelle is here. She hasn't come out of the girls' locker room yet.

"Scab, what'd you do to your toe?" Doyle asks.

I retie the string of my swim trunks. "I . . . uh . . . tripped in the water trap while trying to set a new record on the Mighty Maze."

"Tough nuggets." He leans over to examine the big toe on my right foot. I edge back a little to make sure he doesn't get *too* close of a look. Doyle knows me from the bones out.

Lewis Pigford stops picking his nose. "Wicked toe, Scab." He sounds jealous.

Kids from our class are circling me. Emma winces. "Is it broken?"

"Can you bend it?" Juan wants to know.

"Does it hurt?" asks Henry.

I ignore the first two questions and answer no to
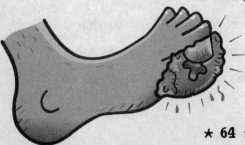 Henry's, which is the truth. My real big toe, under the painted clay toe I'm wearing,

★ 64 ★

⋆ SCAB'S TRICK TOE ⋆

⋆ One cap from a tube of pump toothpaste (or any cap
   that fits snugly over your toe)

⋆ One mound of clay the same color as your skin

⋆ Glue

⋆ Red, green, purple, and black acrylic paint

⋆ One self-adhesive bandage strip

⋆ Pencil

Cover the cap in clay and shape it to look like the big toe
you want to cover. Etch in a toenail and joint ridges using
a pencil tip. Let the clay harden. Paint your toe with red,
green, purple, and black paint to make it look bloody, bruised,
and infected. Go heavy on the green to really creep out the
girls. Glue the toe on over your real toe and secure with the
bandage. When you walk, don't forget to limp!

is fine. I can't take credit for the whole brilliant plan.
It was mostly Joe's idea. Yesterday, after he got tired of
warming my toes, my pup started gnawing on them.

I was trying to wrestle my foot away from him before he drew blood, when it hit me: a trick toe! Talk about the perfect solution. Who is going to want to get into the pool with someone who's got a swollen, bloody, bruised toe? Answer: nobody! It took me most of last night to make the thing. But it was worth the effort. This plan will definitely keep me out of the Deep End. Just looking at the trick toe makes my stomach do a back flip and *I* know it's not real. I love my dog! I've got to remember to thank Isabelle. After all, she is the one who convinced my parents that I was responsible enough to take care of a dog. Every now and then it turns out my sister is good for something. Who knew?

By the way, where *is* my sister?

Ashlynn sees my foot. "Oh, Scab. That looks terrible. Are you in pain?"

"I'm okay," I say bravely.

"Is it infected?" calls Cloey. Her orange flip-flops are going *splick-splack*, *splick-splack* as she rushes this way. Her mother is peering over the railing of the bleachers where the parents sit. Cloey waves a pink towel. "You shouldn't get in the water if it's infected. He shouldn't get in the water, Ashlynn . . ."

Our teacher nods. "I'm afraid you'll have to sit this one out, Scab."

I let my shoulders droop. "O-kay." This is *too* easy.

"Sorry," says Ashlynn. "Also, I'll need a note from your doctor giving you the all-clear to swim next time."

Sweet! My trick toe could get me out of two, maybe three, classes.

SECRETS OF THE MALE SALMON*
⋆ AN ORIGINAL POEM BY SALVATORE W. MCNALLY ⋆

Juan pees in the swimming pool,
Lewis flings snot in there too.
Doyle throws in earwax balls,
Henry pops a zit or two.
With all the stuff we're tossing in,
It's a wonder anyone can swim!

*Don't tell the girls.

My teacher blows her whistle. "Salmon, in the shallow end, please. Scab, you can sit by the edge and learn the breaststroke on dry land, all right?"

"If I have to," I say, my voice oozing disappointment. Brilliant *and* a good actor.

"And whatever you do, Scab, keep your flip-flops *on*," says Cloey. She takes a wide path around me like I'm contagious.

There's Isabelle! Finally. She's barreling straight for me. "My strap broke, and I had to get a safety pin—what's wrong? Why aren't you in the water?" She sounds like our mother.

I cover my trick toe with my left foot. "I banged my foot. Ashlynn said I should stay out of the pool today—"

"Let me see it." She's Mom again.

NO! I want to shout it, but I can't. Kids are watching. Parents are watching. Teachers are watching. Isabelle kneels in front of me. She reaches out. I grimace. Any second now she is going to discover my secret. Her hand is inches from my fake toe—

"Isabelle?"

Thank you, Ashlynn!

"Join the rest of the Salmon in the water, please."

Slowly, Isabelle stands up. She doesn't say anything, but she also doesn't take her gaze off me as she backs away toward the pool.

After warm-ups, Ashlynn shows the class how to do the circular arm movements and breathing for the breaststroke. Push arms outward. Head down. Pull arms inward and underneath the chin. Bring head and shoulders above the water. Breathe. Start again. Arms out. Head down. Arms in. Head and shoulders up. Breathe. It's easy. At least, on land.

"Cloey, don't throw your arms out quite so far," says Ashlynn. "Don't forget to come up for air, Beth. . . . Nice, even strokes everyone. . . . Let it flow . . ."

My class spends almost the entire hour in the shallow end. I knew my sister didn't know what she was talking about. I want to kick myself (with my good toe) for wasting my brilliant invention on today's class. Finally, Ashlynn blows her whistle. "Salmon, swim to the middle ladder. Line up along the edge. Scab, come with me."

I follow her around the pool deck. I almost forget to do the limp. Almost.

When everyone is in place, Ashlynn says, "We're going to learn the frog kick that goes with the breast-stroke. Think about how a frog uses its legs and you'll get this in no time." Standing, Ashlynn lifts one leg, moves it outward in a circle, and brings it back to the middle. "That's all there is to it, except that you are going to use both legs. Scab, you don't have to—"

"I can do it," I say. I collapse onto the concrete on my stomach. I do the frog kick exactly the way Ashlynn showed us.

"Great," says my teacher. "Everybody, watch Scab. That's what you want—a strong, steady snap to help you glide through the water."

"Scab, say, 'Ribbit, ribbit,'" hollers Lewis.

Everyone laughs. I don't care. I like having the class watch me. And look at me go. Push out to make a circle. Then snap. And together. Push out.

Snap. And together. Isabelle, eat my tidal wave! I put my arms and legs together and do the whole stroke. When Ashlynn sees how well I can do it,

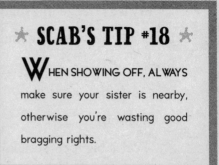

she'll want the whole class to watch me again.

Push out. Snap. And together.

Is Ashlynn watching?

Push out. Snap. And together.

Is Isabelle watching?

Push out. Snap. And—

"Eeeeeeeeewwwww!"

I scrape my chin against the cement. What was that awful noise? I look around. Everybody else is looking around too—everybody except Cloey. Probably because she is the one screaming. Cloey is thrashing her arms all over the place in a very unbreaststroke-like way. She's pointing to something, but I don't see any—

My legs freeze midsnap. I squint. There *is* something in the water. It looks a bit familiar, almost like . . .

Can it be?

Wuh-oh.

"Scab's big toe!" shrieks Cloey.

I swing my head around. My trick toe is gone, all right.

"Where is it?" shouts Juan.

"There! In the water by Emma—"

"*Aggggghhhh!*"

"Everybody out of the pool!"

Suddenly people are splashing and fighting and kicking to get away from the purple-red-green-black blob bobbing among them in the waves.

I try to right myself, which isn't easy. I'm a potato bug on its back.

Isabelle gulps water as she thrashes. "My brother's toe!"

"I'll get it," calls Ashlynn above the hysterics. "Clear the way!"

"No!" I yell, but nobody is listening.

Ashlynn dives in. For a small girl, she sure makes a big splash. I get drenched.

Kids are flinging themselves over the side of the pool. Arms and legs are everywhere. I get kicked in the back. Everything goes dark. A towel is covering my head. *Splick-splack, splick-splack.* I hear Cloey's flip-flops running by. "We're all going to die of infection," she screams at the top of her lungs. "Scab's toe is going to kill us all!"

CHAPTER
7

Fish Tales
(With Extra Tartar Sauce)

y mother is glaring at me in the rear-view mirror. I hunch down, but it is no use. I can't escape her icy gaze. That mirror is huge. After a few minutes of arctic silence, my mother asks the question no kid on Earth can answer. "Salvatore Wallingford McNally, what were you thinking?"

I tap my heels against the bottom of the seat. "I don't know."

Isabelle is in the seat next to me. She is studying me. Her lips are screwed up on one side of her cheek. It's the same face she makes when she's working on a tough math problem. I look out the window. I sure wish Joe were here.

Part of me wants to tell the truth. But I know what will happen if I do. My mother will start quoting Eleanor Roosevelt. She will say, "You gain strength, courage, and confidence by every experience in which you really stop to look fear in the face." She will make me go back to the pool. Parents are big on forcing you to do things that scare the beans out of you. I don't want to stop and look fear in the face. I want to run the other way. So I don't tell her the real reason for making my trick toe. Instead I say, "Swim lessons are lame."

"It's important for you to learn how to swim."

"I *know* how to swim." In the shallow end.

"Let's hope so, Scab, because they are talking about banning you from Little Creek for good."

"Banning him?" Isabelle springs forward. "They can't do that. It was a harmless joke—"

"A harmless joke?" My mother takes a hard left into the driveway of Captain McGillicutty's Fish

SCAB'S MYSTERIES ★ OF THE UNIVERSE ★

HOW IS IT THAT NO MATTER WHERE SHE IS in the world, your mom knows the second you . . .

★ chug milk straight from the carton?

★ break a window?

★ forget to wash your belly button?

★ feed your limp broccoli to the dog?

★ spill *anything* on the carpet?

Another unsolved mystery of the universe!

House. My sister and I grab our door handles and hang on. My mom swings the SUV into the drive-through. We are in line behind two cars. "Let's take a body count, shall we?"

I slide down a little more.

"Poor Emma Wilkins fainted on the pool deck. Henry Mapanoo is on his way to the doctor to have that gash in his arm looked at. Beth Burwell twisted her ankle—thank goodness she's all right. And did I mention that Mrs. Zittle is making them clean the pool because Cloey is convinced that was your *real* toe? They are going to have to drain the pool from top to bottom . . . ?"

Isabelle leans over to me while our mother goes on. "It *was* a joke, wasn't it?"

"Of course," I hiss. "What else would it be?"

She is looking at my feet. They seem to be twitching without my knowledge.

I make them stop. It's not easy.

". . . we can only hope banning you from the pool

is the worst they do." My mother is still talking. She inches the car forward. "We'll be lucky if we don't get sued."

"Sorry," I mumble. I hadn't meant for things to get so crazy. But, on the up side, I did accomplish my goal. If I am banned from the pool, I certainly can't take lessons. No lessons, no Deep End. No Deep End, no problem.

"No swimming lessons, no fishing this summer," corrects my mom.

I am about to protest, when it hits me: I did not say that out loud! Bug spit! My mother can read my mind.

I fly up. "You promised I could go fishing with Uncle Ant if I took the Salmon class—"

"I said you could go if you *passed* the class. There's a big difference."

"But Mom, that's no—"

"Scab, if I were you, I would choose my words very carefully right now. Your father and I have yet to discuss your punishment for this stunt."

I flop back in my seat.

"What if he said he was sorry?" asks Isabelle. "You know, what if he said it to the whole class? They'd have to let him back in then, wouldn't they?"

My mother throws her hands up. "Who knows?"

Isabelle faces me. "Scab, just say you are sorry—"

"No." I fold my arms. "Why should I?"

"So you can come back to class."

"Who says I want to come back?"

My mom rolls the SUV forward. Finally we are at the enormous anchor that holds up the menu board. A green octopus crackles with static. "Aye, aye, matey, welcome to Captain McGillicutty's Fish House. May I take your order?"

My mom leans out her window. "We'll take a halibut special with extra tartar sauce, a two-piece fish basket with fries . . ."

"Don't forget the chowder, Mom," says Isabelle. She elbows me and whispers, "I know you want to go back."

"Do not."

"Do so."

I grit my teeth. "Do *not*."

She looks down. My knee is jiggling. I make it stop. My sister grins. "Do so."

"Meow, meow."

Joe lifts his head from my chest.

"Meow, meow."

"It's the secret doorbell," I remind him.

I rigged it up last year after I got grounded for building a flying saucer. I made it out of one of the hubcaps from my dad's SUV, Isabelle's ladybug headband, and the garage door opener. I'd show you how, but I'm already grounded for three weeks thanks to my trick toe. Plus, my spaceship never did work right. Now neither does our garage door.

I built the doorbell to stay in touch with Doyle while I'm on restriction. The meowing is coming from one of my sister's old stuffed animals, a yellow cat named Abalard. He's missing one eye and most of his fur, but he still talks. To make my doorbell, I gathered a bunch of stuff—Abalard, a gumball machine, some dominos—what else? Oh, and my plastic apatosaurus dinosaur, Ralph. He got his name after spewing toxic applesauce in a wrestling match with Barbie's little sister, Kelly. Boy, did Isabelle go nuclear over that. I guess applesauce and doll hair are not a good combo.

SCAB'S SECRET DOORBELL
★ HOW IT WORKS ★

WHEN YOU TUG ON THE PING-PONG PADDLE, IT jerks on the cable, which pulls down the handle of the gumball machine on the inside of my windowsill, which releases a megamarble, which knocks over a row of seven dominoes, which hits my mini red Ferrari 250 LM racer, sending it down the racetrack into a wall of blocks, which collapses into a bucket, which tips to release Ralph the apatosaurus (now glued to a skateboard), who rolls down a ruler over a hill of comics and smashes into my mom's cookbook, Smile and Say Goat Cheese!, which falls and lands on Abalard's right paw, which causes him to do one of three things: meow, purr, or cough up a furball.

Even after a couple dozen shampoos, Kelly still looks like she got sucked into an F5 tornado.

Anyway, I connected everything together (see my notebook). To hook up the actual doorbell, I tossed an old computer cable out my window. I ran it down the corner of the house and tucked it behind the drainpipe. I wrapped the cord around a Ping-Pong paddle, hiding it behind the bayberry bushes. Now all Doyle has to do is crawl through the bushes, find the Ping-Pong paddle, and tug! Less than a minute later, Abalard lets me know my best friend is outside. Sweet, huh?

It's Saturday morning, about ten o'clock. On my way to the window, I grab Ralph to reset the doorbell. Looking outside, I see fishing poles and tackle boxes littering our side yard. My stomach twists into a cinch knot—that's what we use to tie fishing hook to the line. It's killing me not to be able to go fishing with the guys. Yesterday I gave Doyle the recipe to my Fish Buffet Bait so the two of them could go after the—whatever it is—in Beeson's Lake. I really wanted to tell him the truth about what I saw, but I didn't. I couldn't. He'd think I'm a Fruit Roll-Up. So Joe and I have made a pact to forget we ever saw that long, leathery brown neck slip under the water. I open my window. Joe sticks his head out and barks at Will and Doyle.

"Shhhhhhh." I pull him to me. "How'd it go?" I whisper loudly, but not too loudly. I am not supposed to be talking to my friends at all while I'm grounded unless I am at school. Isabelle's room is next to mine. If her supersensitive dolphin ears are nearby, it'll be another week tacked on to my month in jail.

"We didn't catch Zenobia," Doyle hisses. "But something is—"

"Ze-what?"

"Zenobia," says Will. "That's what we named the big fish."

Doyle bobs his head. "Except there's—"

"You named it?"

Will grins. "Uh-huh. Zenobia. Doyle's idea."

"Why?"

"I don't know—it didn't look like a Steve," flips Doyle. "I have a great-aunt Zenobia with spooky, big fish eyes, okay? If you'd zip it for a minute and let me finish."

With one quick motion I zip my lips.

"Something weird is going on at Beeson's Lake."

Instant goose bumps. No need to add water. I take a breath. "Weird how?"

My best friend scratches his head. "You're going to think we're Fruit Roll-Ups."

Now I've got to know. "I won't." I hold my hand up to swear.

"We saw something," croaks Doyle, looking around nervously.

★ ENORMOUS APATOSAURUS ★

THE APATOSAURUS WAS ONE OF THE LARGEST animals ever to roam the Earth! This plant-eating dinosaur lived more than 130 million years ago. With its sweeping tail, long neck, and tiny head it looked like a giant lizard; the word Apatosaurus means "deceptive lizard." Its brain was barely the size of an apple! Many of these dinosaur fossils have been found in western North America (gulp). Scientists figure the average life span of an apatosaurus was about one hundred years. But they don't know for sure (double gulp).

★ APATOSAURUS FACTS ★

- ★ Weight: up to thirty tons
- ★ Height: up to thirty feet
- ★ Head to tail length: up to ninety feet (thirty-foot tail, twenty-foot neck, two-foot head)

"Yeah?" I say coolly, real coolly, as a thousand new goose bumps pop to life on the back of my neck.

"I don't know exactly—this thing." He stretches his arms out. "And it had this kind of thing . . . with a long thing and a tiny thing. . . . I can't describe it exactly. . . ."

"It looked round, kind of like a beach ball," blurts Will. "A brown beach ball with a neck and a big tail—"

Did he say it? Did he actually say the word?

He did! He did say it!

"No, no, no," says Doyle. "It was more of an oval . . . like a football . . . and it had a long tail like a dragon, but it wasn't a dragon. . . . It looked like . . . like . . ." His hands are flying all over the place.

"Like that," blurts Will. He is pointing up. He is pointing up at my dog.

I laugh. "Joe? Zenobia looked like Joe?"

"No." He moves his finger to the right. "Like *that*."

He can't mean it. Not *this*? I lift up my plastic apatosaurus.

This time there is no arguing. Both of my friends are nodding.

So am I.

CHAPTER

8

D-Day

I'm very, very, very, very sorry about my . . . uh . . . prank last week." I twist my towel into a knot. My entire swimming class is standing around me in a circle. "Thanks for letting me come back," I say, digging my toe into a small hole in the cement. "I never meant for anyone to get hurt."

I give Henry the same sad eyes Joe gives me when I leave for school. I really *am* sorry that Henry tripped in the stampede to escape my floating toe and had to get two stitches in his elbow. Henry grins. "I'm okay."

Juan, Emma, and most of the other kids are grinning too. Not Cloey. The only thing smiling on that girl are about two dozen yellow happy faces on her white swimsuit. Orange flip-flops are thumping against concrete.

"Thank you, Scab," says Ashlynn. She claps her hands twice. "Okay, Salmon, in the water, please. We've got a lot of work to do today."

Doyle bounces over to me while we are practicing the breaststroke arms. "So what are we going to do?"

"Do?" I'm making smooth, flowing circles. Is Ashlynn watching?

"You know, about Beeson's—"

"Not now."

"Geez, Scab, we just discovered there's a dinosaur living in the lake. How can you do nothing?"

"Shhhh, will you? I never said I wasn't going to do anything. I said, 'Not *now*.'"

★ SCAB'S TIP #3 ★

WHEN SAYING YOU'RE SORRY, always use at least three *very*'s so people know you mean it, unless you are apologizing to a girl. She doesn't care how many *very*'s you use 'cause she doesn't want your apology anyway. She wants you to suffer. She wants you to get a gross, gooey, pulsating rash on your butt.

"Then you do have a plan—?"

"Of course." Don't I always?

"Wouldn't it be cool if you invented something for us to use to catch him?" He sees the look on my face. "You did! You did invent something! What is it? How does it work? Can I be in charge of the marshmallows?"

"Who said anything about marshmallows?"

"Most of your inventions lately have *something* to do with marshmallows."

I think about it and realize he is right.

Doyle moves in. "So what are we going to do about Zenobia?"

"Once my grounding is lifted we'll—"

"What's a Zenobia?" Lewis is beside us.

★ **DID YOU EVER WONDER . . .** ★

HOW MANY MINI MARSHMALLOWS A KID CAN STUFF in his mouth at one time?

Answer: twenty-four (twenty-eight when I had no front teeth)

"Noth—" I don't even get the word out before Doyle starts spilling his guts.

"It's this dinosaur we found in Beeson's Lake."

"That's a good one, Doyle," I hoot. "Ha! He's just joking." I smack Doyle in the shoulder with my circling arm.

Slowpoke finally gets it. "Um . . . yeah . . . I was only joking."

"A dinosaur, huh?" Lewis rubs his nose. "Beeson's Lake? Maybe I'll go out there this weekend and check it out for myself."

I snort. "It's your time. Waste it if you want."

Bug spit! Thanks to my best friend, we're going to have to put my plan into action right away. We're going to catch that dinosaur, all right. But not in the way Doyle thinks. That's all I can say right now.

"Salmon out of the water, please," calls Ashlynn. We still have ten minutes left in class. "Form a line on the pool deck," she says, so I figure we are going to play a game. I figure wrong.

Ashlynn tells Isabelle, who's at the head of the

line (naturally), to follow her. It takes me about a second to realize *where* we are going. And when I do, I stop cold.

Doyle bashes into me. "The deep end!" He blasts. "Cooooool." My best friend pushes me forward.

Everybody starts chattering.

"Do you think we'll get to jump off the high dive?" Beth turns around to ask me.

I just stare at her.

"I hope so!" squeals Cloey from the back.

As we walk, the water gets bluer and bluer. Deeper and deeper. My body starts to tingle. Bluer and bluer. Deeper and deeper. Before I know it, we are there. I want to run, but I can't. I have no feeling from the dancing squirrels down.

"Did everyone learn to do a kneeling dive in Guppy class?" Ashlynn asks. "Raise your hand if you did."

Isabelle's hand shoots up. Henry, Doyle, Cloey, Juan, and Beth lift theirs, too. Lewis, Emma, and I slowly put ours in the air because we don't want to look like idiots. My hand is lying. I've never dived

THINGS I LEARNED
★ IN GUPPY CLASS ★

★ If your teacher says "dude" more than twenty-eight times a minute, you're probably not going to learn much about swimming. You will, however, learn what a fakie is (Someone who pretends to know a lot about surfing but really doesn't, dude!).

★ Always hold your nose when doing an underwater back flip or a cannonball jump, or when following Lewis out of the locker room.

★ It's pretty easy to dive to the bottom of the shallow end and pick up a purple jawbreaker. It isn't so easy getting the purple candy dye off your hands and arms and legs and feet.

★ Always tell the lifeguard *before* you try to break the world record for holding your breath while floating facedown.

before. I *was* in the Guppy class, but my teacher, Todd, wasn't very strict. Or smart. He never caught on that every time we practiced kneeling dives, I had to race to the locker room to pee.

Ashlynn is showing us how to do a kneeling dive. She is using Isabelle as an example. Naturally. Isabelle will do it perfectly.

"Knees at the edge," she says to my sister. "Arms above your head. Hands together with your palms flat. Right fingers over left to make a pointed triangle. Good. Now lock your thumb under your palm. Head down. Remember, you're going to lead into the water with your fingertips, Isabelle. Imagine your fingers going in first, then your arms, head, and body. I'll hold your waist and guide you, okay?"

"Okay."

"Bend and relax. Take a breath. Go whenever you're ready."

Isabelle leans forward and easily goes into the water. That didn't look so hard. A second later, my sister's head pops to the surface. "Can I do it again?"

"One to a customer today. We're almost out of time and I want everyone to have a chance. Salmon, each of you take your dive, then head for the showers. Henry, you're up."

I count back. After Henry it's Juan, Emma, Lewis, Beth, then me.

What am I so worried about? I am, after all, the Mighty Maze king. I've done stuff that was a million trillion times scarier than this. All I have to do is stay close to the edge. Dive in, swim up, and reach out. The edge will be right there. A kneeling dive will be a snap. Not even that. Half a snap—a "sn." That's how simple it will be.

Henry goes into the water doing an impression of an ironing board. *Splat!*

"Belly flop," announces Lewis.

The class snickers. There are four people between the Deep End and me. Forget the snaps. My stomach aches. Juan kneels down for his dive. I step out of line. "You can go ahead," I say to Doyle.

"Thanks," he says.

"Go ahead," I say to Cloey.

"No, thanks."

"What do you mean?" I make a move to go behind her.

She blocks me. "I mean, '*No, thanks.*'"

"W . . . why not?"

"I want to go last."

"That's stupid." I try to step around her, but she keeps scooting back so I can't.

"If it's so stupid, why do you want to go last?" Cloey sticks her elbow out.

I push it down. "I just do."

"So do I. And I was here first. I mean, last." She pushes her palm against my chest. I slap it away.

Before I know it, we are two sumo wrestlers in a championship match—each of us trying to shove the other toward the pool. For a stick figure in a happy-face suit, Cloey is awfully strong. Cloey twists my arm behind me, but I get away. I lock on to her wrists, but she gets away. Time is running out. Ashlynn is helping Beth set up for her dive.

A pain tears through my calf. Cloey has kicked me! "Ow!" I yelp. I release my hold, which gives the Stick-Figure Gladiator time to get into a firm stance—legs out, knees bent, back arched. This time, she isn't budging.

Splash! Beth is in the pool. Doyle is next. Then me.

If I don't do something soon . . .

I look at the water. It's so blue. I have to look away.

Do something! ANYTHING!

I spin away from Cloey and start walking as fast as I can toward the boys' locker room. I trot past the chipped sign that says no running. Okay, I confess. I am running.

Someone is calling me.

I don't look back. I don't stop. Instead, I shout, "GOT TO PEE."

It isn't a lie. My bladder is about three seconds away from exploding—a new world record.

Isabelle Smells Something Fishy (Wuh-oh)

I rip a long stem out of the dirt. I wonder if it is a weed. I smell it. It doesn't stink. Yep, it's a weed. I toss it into the bucket. Joe thinks it is something to play with and tips the bucket over trying to get at it. Silly dog.

My mom likes to grow lavender, thyme, and lots of other smelly plants in her herb garden. I like the mints best—spearmint, orange mint, pineapple mint (it *really* smells like pineapple). Waldorf likes the mints too. His favorite is catmint, probably because he is a cat. Waldorf is a fluffy white-and-gray Maine coon. I've never been to Maine, but they must have huge cats. Waldorf weighs nineteen pounds. He belongs to the Dawbers next door.

When Waldorf thinks no one is looking, he sneaks into our herb garden. He flops on his back in the catmint. My mom doesn't know he does this. She blames Joe for squashing her catmint.

Waldorf is hiding in the bushes. He's waiting for Joe and me to leave. He's not the only one watching us. My sister is supposed to be watering the tulips, but she has been spying on me for the last ten minutes. I hate to tell her, but she's been watering our concrete patio for eight of those ten minutes. Joe circles me,

---

★ BIG CAT, BIG LEGEND ★

THE MAINE COON'S BUSHY TAIL AND RACCOONLIKE colors sparked the myth that the cat was a cross between a longhair cat and a raccoon. Not true. Can't be done. More likely, the breed is a cross between American shorthair cats and Norwegian forest cats brought by the Vikings (the early peoples from Scandinavia, not the football team from Minnesota). Maine coons remain playful and kittenlike, even after they grow up to be big (VERY big) adults.

sniffing all over the place like he's on the trail of something good. He must smell Waldorf. Joe actually likes cats, especially Waldorf. He is always trying to get him to play. Joe takes off running through the yard, then turns to see if Waldorf is chasing him. He isn't, of course. Waldorf is nineteen pounds. He isn't chasing anything.

"I don't get you," Isabelle finally says to me.

I keep pulling weeds.

"Something's not right."

I keep pulling weeds. It's not a good idea to encourage her. Not that keeping quiet will shut her up. Nothing does.

"I keep wondering why you made that trick toe."

See?

"I told you it was a prank," I say.

"That's what I can't figure out." She turns off the water and walks over to me. "I always know what you're up to, Scab, because you always give it away."

"Do not."

"Do so. When you're pulling a practical joke, you do that bobbing thing with your eyebrows."

I grunt. I do not bob. Do I?

"It's true. You bob. You *always* bob." Isabelle edges closer. So does Waldorf. "But on the day you wore your trick toe, your eyebrows didn't move. Not once. I watched you. You actually looked—I don't know— scared."

I dig out another weed. "I was not."

But she isn't listening. "Then the other day when you apologized to the Salmon, you couldn't stop squirming."

"So?"

"So you only fidget when you're lying, Scab."

I sit back on my heels. "I wasn't lying. I *was* sorry about what happened to Henry and everybody—"

"I know that." She bends down. She peers at me over the bluish purple stalks of purple catmint. "I meant you were lying when you told the class it was a prank."

I start hacking at the ground with my weeder, even though I am at the end of the row and there are no weeds left.

"It wasn't a prank, was it, Scab?" Isabelle asks softly.

There's *got* to be a weed here somewhere.

"You know what I think?" asks my sister. "I think you were trying to get out of class on purpose. I think you wanted people to think your toe was really hurt. I think—"

I give her a ripper snort. "You've got to quit standing so close to the oven when you're making those rock muffins of yours, 'cause your brain is fried."

She ignores me. "I also think you were trying to get out of diving the other day. That's why you ran for the locker room like your squirrel buns were on fire."

Bug spit! I thought Isabelle was in the girls' locker room when I made my escape.

My sister breaks off a piece of orange mint and sticks it in her mouth. "What I can't figure out is why. Why would you try to get out of swimming when you know it means you won't get to go on Uncle Ant's boat this summer?"

I bang my weeder against the bucket.

BEWARE OF ISABELLE'S ★ ROCK MUFFINS! ★

NEVER EAT MY SISTER'S CRANBERRY-CHERRY-peach-raisin-walnut-cinnamon muffins. Once, my dad broke a tooth on one. My sister's rock muffins come in handy for other stuff besides taking your teeth out. You can use them as bowling pins, skipping stones (especially the burnt ones with the flat tops), rocket launch pads, car-wash sponges, baseballs, and dog toys (don't worry; even Joe knows better than to eat them).

She twists the mint in her mouth. "What's going on, Scab?" It's not a demand. For once, it's just a question.

I lift my head. We both have the same blue eyes sprinkled with gray dots. We both have a single dimple on the left side of our mouths. I want to tell her, but I don't want to tell her. If I tell Isabelle the truth, she'll tattle. If I don't tell, I'll have to keep carrying this secret around by myself. And it's starting to get heavy. I don't know what to do. For a minute I think it sure would be nice to tell *someone*, but . . .

"There's nothing going on," I hear myself say. "Nothing."

I can't do it.

Isabelle flings her chewed-up mint into my bucket. She goes to wind up the hose. I pick up my bucket. I whistle for Joe. We head around the side of the house so I can dump my weeds in the compost bin. My shoulder hurts.

I look down at my dog. "I did the right thing, didn't I?"

He looks up at me.

"Yeah, but if I trusted her, she'd only go blabbing to everyone."

Joe butts his head against my leg.

Maybe he's right. What if Isabelle didn't tattle? What if she could help? What if she could think of a way for me to stay out of the Deep End and still go fishing with my uncle?

I drop my bucket. "Isabelle!" I race down the gravel path. Joe follows, then passes me on the straight-away. Four feet are so much faster than two! I take the corner, skidding all the way. "Isabelle, I changed my . . ."

The backyard is empty. The hose is neatly coiled against the house. Everything is still, except for the *drip-drip-drip* of the leaky spigot. And my mother's catmint. It is moving. I count one, two, three, four gray-and-white paws swaying with the feathery, purple stems. In the dirt a fluffy, white tummy wriggles. Joe is tearing full speed across the grass toward the catmint, eager to play. I put my fingers in my mouth and let out a whistle. Joe pulls up and circles back to me. "Sit. Good boy. Now, if you'd only do that at the lake, we'd be set."

Waldorf is no longer wallowing happily in the mint. He has flipped over. He's hunched down, his chin touching the dirt. Golden eyes stare into mine. He doesn't trust us with his secret.

"It's all right, Waldorf," I say. "We won't tell."

10

The Dino Hunters

Inch by endless inch, I slide open my bedroom window.

Eeeeeeeak!

I freeze. Miss Dolphin Ears is snoring up a thunderstorm next door, but it doesn't take much to wake her. It's five thirty on Saturday morning. I'm going out my escape hatch to meet Doyle and Will at Beeson's Lake.

I know, I know. I'm still grounded. But what choice do I have? We can't let Lewis Pigford get there ahead of us. We can't let him find Zenobia first.

I climb out my window and gently push it closed. It doesn't creak this time. I scoot on my butt down the sloping roof to the edge. Whoa! The house is spinning. Or is it the yard that's twirling? Don't look down. I reach out for the oak tree. I've got one foot on a branch and am bringing the other leg across when—

Rrrrrrrrrrrrrrrip.

This is not a sound you want to hear when you are twenty feet up. I keep going, only turning around to look when I am in the tree.

Bug spit! Half of my back pocket is dangling from a nail sticking out of the gutter. Could I have left a bigger clue for Isabelle?

There's no time to go back. I scamper down the oak tree and snag my backpack from under the rhododendron bush (where I hid it last night). I flip up the hood of my sweatshirt to cover my head. Hunching over, I carefully, but quickly, pick my way across the yard. In my green sweatshirt I blend in with the grass.

I am stealth. I look left.

I am indestructible. I look right.

I am—

—being watched.

Joe!

Through the window of the back door, two dark brown eyes are begging me to let him come. I can tell by the way his mouth is half open he is whimpering. It's killing me to leave him, but I have no choice. This isn't our usual lazy day of fishing. I have to focus all of my energy on catching Zenobia. I won't have time to toss a stick or run after him if he starts chasing ducks. I can't take him. I just can't. Not today. As I slip past the back door, I put my finger to my lips. "Shhhhh. Next time, okay? I promise."

He closes his mouth. Good dog. He understands. I keep tiptoeing across the backyard. I put my hand on the gate latch—

"Woof."

I hold. I count to ten.

Please, Joe. Please understand. I can't take you.

Nothing.

Good dog. Okay, let's try this again.

I slowly lift the latch.

"Woof. Woof."

I run. Not through the gate but back toward the house. I jam my key in the lock and throw open the door. Joe comes bounding out. I shut the door. We take off down the street. Before we cross the intersection, I glance over my shoulder. There are no lights on at my house. Big relief.

"You're late," says the willow tree guarding the path to Beeson's Lake.

"Sorry," I reply to the lazy branches.

Doyle steps out from behind the thick trunk. He's carrying his fishing pole and tackle box. "I didn't think you were coming."

"Arf," barks Joe as if to say, 'Me neither.' I pat his head. Bug spit! In all of the rush, I forgot to grab Joe's leash. "Stay with me, you hear?" I say firmly. "Stay with me." I look around. "Where's Will?"

"Paper route. He'll meet us there."

I yawn. "Lewis?"

Doyle smirks. "No sign of him."

When we get to the lake, I pick a spot on the west side opposite the tippy dock. I inspect the water to make sure there aren't any big rocks in the way. "This is it," I say, opening my backpack. "This is our launch site."

"What are we launching?"

I lift my new invention out of my pack.

"A toy submarine?"

"Scab's Surveillance Submersible." I pop the top off my yellow model submarine.

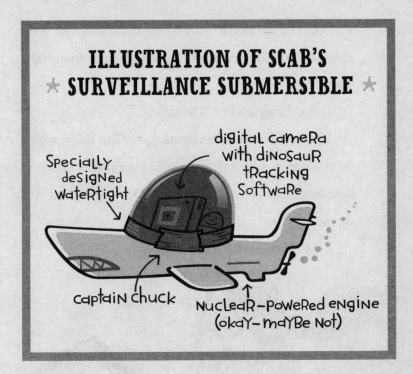

ILLUSTRATION OF SCAB'S
★ SURVEILLANCE SUBMERSIBLE ★

digital camera
with dinosaur
tracking
software

Specially
designed
watertight

captain chuck

Nuclear-powered engine
(okay- maybe not)

"You got a Weeble in there for a pilot?" laughs
Doyle.

I do not laugh. "Inside the submersible is my
specially rigged digital camera," I say seriously, which
shuts him up. "Once I push this button, it will snap a
photo every thirty seconds for one hour. The photos

will then be wirelessly sent to my computer. We'll be able to study the images when we get back to my lab. Clear?"

Doyle bites his lip. "Clear."

I flip on the remote control, set the boat in the murky water, and wait for Doyle's countdown. But it doesn't come. When I look back, Doyle is kicking the moss off a log.

I stand up. "What's the matter?"

"When you said we were going to catch Zenobia, I didn't think you meant with a camera."

"What *did* you think?"

"I thought we were going to do it with a net or something."

"Catch a dinosaur? With a net?"

"Or something. I bet that's what Lewis would do."

"Yeah, I bet that snotball would," I mutter. "Look, Doyle, whatever's in the lake, it already broke my fishing pole. And if it is an eighty-foot apatosaurus, do you think a net is going to hold him?"

He shoves his hands in his pockets. "I don't know."

"But this"—I hold up the sub—"will get us proof that Zenobia exists."

"Uh-huh." He's still taking it out on the moss.

"If we get a good shot, I'll bet they'll print it in the *Granite Falls Gazette*." I dig around in my backpack. "They'll probably do a story about how we found Zenobia and interview us and everything. We'll be famous—"

"Famous?" He catches the bag of mini marsh-mallows I toss to him. "What's this for?"

"Zenobia liked them the first time around, so I figured we'd try again." A ray of light slices the trees in half. The sun is coming up. If we're going to do this, we have to do it now. "Come on, Doyle," I say. "It's the best we've got. You bait your hook and I'll run the submersible and let's just see what happens, okay?"

He gives me a slow grin. "Okay."

I hold up my hand. "Did you hear that?"

"Where's Joe?"

"Here." I point to my dog, who is sniffing around a log. I haven't taken my eyes off of him the whole time we've been here. I sure wish I had that leash.

"Somebody's coming. It must be Will—"

"Or Lewis." I shove the sub under my sweatshirt. Doyle stuffs the bag of marshmallows down his pants. Why he does this, I have no idea. We aren't trying to hide snacks from Lewis. We hear whistling. Relax. It's okay. Only one person whistles "Jingle Bells" in the middle of May.

"You almost missed the launch," Doyle says when Will steps through the tall grass. He taps his watch. "I'm setting my timer for one hour. T minus ten seconds to launch."

I race to the water, juggling the remote, the submersible, and a roll of duct tape. "Wait!"

"You know the rules. Can't stop the launch count once it's started. Nine . . ."

USES FOR EVERY INVENTOR'S
★ #1 TOOL: DUCT TAPE ★

★ Patches the rip in your jeans you got when you went through the Mighty Maze (don't tell my mom).

★ Reattaches the tail of your sister's plastic horse, Sugar Pie, which may have accidentally broken off while he was bungee jumping from your bedroom window (baaaaad horsie).

★ Wrap it around a yardstick (sticky side out) so you can pick up coins behind the couch.

★ Makes a watertight seal for your dino-hunting submersible!

I push the automatic shutter on the camera. I snap the top onto the submersible.

". . . eight . . . seven . . . six . . ."

I wrap duct tape around the top seam twice to make a watertight seal. I rip the duct tape off with my teeth. Ouch!

". . . five . . . four . . . three . . ."

I set the submersible in the water and pick up the remote control unit.

". . . two . . . one . . ."

My heart pounds in rhythm to the count.

"Dive, Scab! Dive!"

CHAPTER

Deep Water Rescue!

eep. *Beep. Beep.*

It's Doyle's watch. He's fishing off an old tree stump nearby. "Time's up!" he calls.

"Bring it back," I tell Will, who's holding the remote unit. We've been taking turns running my submarine. "I hope we got some clear photos on the computer."

Will lets out a sigh. "Me too."

I know what he means. Swatting away bugs for an hour while Scab's Surveillance Submersible crisscrossed the bottom of the lake wasn't much of an adventure. We wanted to see Zenobia's massive, scaly, brown neck rise out of the water. We wanted to see a thick tail whip through the lily pads. We wanted to hear the roar of an ancient dinosaur echo through the forest. Now that I think about it, maybe it's good those things didn't happen. The only camera I brought is ten feet *under* water.

"Come on, boy." I gently wake Joe, who's been snoozing on a pad of thick, dewy grass. "We're going home. I bet you're hungry." I know *I* am.

"Check this out!" Doyle holds up a scrawny gray minnow.

"Sure took a lot of marshmallows," I tease when I see the empty bag.

"I didn't get breakfast."

I check Doyle's watch. Six minutes after seven. Bug spit! My dad gets up at seven thirty. "I have to get home," I say, turning to Will. "Are you bringing it in?"

He's jerking the toggle. "I'm trying, but it keeps stopping—"

"Here, let me do it." I take the remote unit from

him. I punch the blue button. We wait. We scan the water. It should have been up by now. "Let's split up and start looking."

Doyle and Will trot off in opposite directions down the shoreline.

The power light on the remote is flickering. No! The batteries are dying. My parents will kill me if I lose another digital camera. Don't ask. I hit the blue button again. Come on, surface! *Surface!*

"I see it," shouts Doyle from about fifty yards away. "Over here!"

I pound on the side of the remote as I run for Doyle. Joe is on my heels. Will is on *his* paws. When I get there, my best friend is pointing to a spot about thirty feet offshore. My yellow sub is caught in a clump of lily pads.

"Woof, woof!"

"It's not a duck, Joe," I laugh. "He thinks it's a—"

"Woof, woof!"

"Oh, no, you don't," I say as he pushes past me. I lunge for Joe's collar.

And miss.

My dog charges for the lake.

"No!" I shout. "Joe, don't go in the—"

Ker-splat!

"Joe?" My voice breaks.

"Bring the boat in," orders Doyle. "He'll follow it—"

"I can't. I'm dead," I say, flicking the power switch to prove it.

"Joe! Joe, come back!" We scream, but it's no use.

All we can do is watch the top of his golden head glide through the water as he paddles toward the submarine. Bad dog!

I stick my fingers in my mouth and whistle. Nothing comes out. It wouldn't matter. When Joe has ducks on the brain, nothing works. Wait. Why am I freaking out? Joe loves to play fetch. He will snag the submersible and swim back to shore. Everything is going to work out perfectly, after all. Good dog!

"What's he doing?" asks Doyle.

Joe is close to the sub, but he hasn't grabbed it in his mouth. I'm not sure why. He's treading water. "Come on, boy." I cup my hands over my mouth. "Get the duck and come back.
Get the duck, Joe."

But Joe doesn't take a hold of the sub. Instead, his head dips under the water.

"What's wrong?" asks Will.

"He's okay," I say. My breath is coming faster. My heart is beating harder.

Joe lets out a yelp.

"I think he's stuck," says Doyle.

"Stuck?" I gulp.

"In the lily pads. I think he's stuck in the lily pads."

"What do we do?" asks Will.

I kick off my shoes. I pull off my sweatshirt. Racing down the rocky shore, I hurdle a log and splash out into the lake. When the water hits my knees, I throw my body in headfirst. The cold water sends a jolt through me. I start swimming the crawl stroke. It's my best stroke. I can hear Will and Doyle shouting, telling me to hurry.

I am. I am.

I windmill my arms. I breathe. I stroke. And I kick. I kick hard. Am I moving? I'm not sure. I could be staying in the same place for all I know. I slap the

water, trying to push it behind me. I look ahead. Yes!
I am moving.

Don't forget to breathe.

I keep going. It feels like I am splashing wildly,
kicking forever.

Kick. Stroke. Kick. Stroke. These are the only two
words my brain knows.

I don't feel cold anymore. I see Joe's head. He's
low in the water. I'm almost there. I reach out to pull
my dog to me. He kicks me in the stomach. Water
floods my nose and throat. It tastes like . . .

. . . like what?

Like old sauerkraut and
mud pies and dandelions
and cat litter . . .

Breathe! *Breathe!*

I am coughing. "Easy . . . boy," I choke, spitting out water. I slide my arm down under his legs to feel the thick, intertwining stems of water lilies. "I'm here, Joe. I'm here. I'll get you . . . out of here."

He relaxes. A little. Maybe he knows I won't let him go. Or maybe he's too tired to fight. I bring my legs up as if I am sitting in a chair. Cradling Joe against my knees, I reach down and grab at the lily stalks. I yank again. And again. A cramp slices through my collarbone. This isn't working. I'm going to have to try something else.

"I'll be right . . . back, Joe," I huff. "Keep paddling." I take one big breath to fill my lungs with air. Then I dive. As I go down, I throw my left arm above my head, to help support my dog. With the other arm, I reach out to unravel the stems from his leg. I open my eyes, but it stings. It's dark. And still. And strange. Like slow motion. Like a dream. With bubbles. I grope around, feel for a stalk, and pull on it. I pull again. And again. I can't tell if I'm doing any good. I am running out of air.

Something smacks me in the chin. It's Joe's leg! He's free.

Go! Go! Go!

I break the surface, my mouth open wide. After a few breaths, I take hold of Joe and start swimming for the shore. I use the frog kick and do a half-breaststroke with my right arm while my left arm hangs on to my dog. I hear Ashlynn's voice in my head.

Push out. Nice, even strokes. Just let it flow.

"We're doing good, Joe . . . doing good . . ." I sputter as we close the distance to the beach.

My leg hits something. Or something hits my leg. "Ow!"

"What's wrong?" shouts Doyle.

"Something just . . ."—I gasp—". . . bit me."

"Zenobia!" my friends scream.

"Get out of there," yells Doyle, waving his arms.

Thanks for the advice, buddy.

I tell myself not to panic. But myself isn't exactly listening.

I can feel Joe's lungs going in and out. My shoulders ache. My legs feel as if every last muscle in them has withered and died. We are slowing down. My chin slides into the paisley pattern of green and black algae. I'm so tired.

Don't give up. Keep going. Just let it flow.

My toes are dragging in mud. Thank goodness. Doyle and Will are here. "T . . . take him," I wheeze, sliding Joe into Will's arms.

I start to crumble. Doyle grabs me. On the beach, I drop to my knees. My chest heaves. I can't get enough oxygen. There isn't enough air in the world. "I . . . I . . ."

The sky is twirling. So is the sand. I see streams of blood. It's coming from a gash in my leg.

"Stay here with Will," I hear Doyle say. "I'm going to get your dad."

"O . . . kay."

I know I am going to be in a garbage truck full of trouble. The list of my crimes is a long one.

Sneaking out of the house while grounded.

Losing an expensive model submarine.

Losing my more expensive digital camera.

But none of it makes any difference. Everything that matters is right here. Right now.

I fling a shivering arm around Joe's neck. I bury my head in his wet fur. He licks my ear, then my whole face. Will doesn't say anything. He lets me rest. And he lets me cry. And for that I am glad. I don't let go of Joe until my dad comes for us.

12

Raisins and Realizations

Scab?"

Joe yawns. He's beside me, his head on my airplane pillow.

I slap my comic book over my face. "Shoo. Scram. Esca-*lator*," I say.

"I brought you peanut butter and celery sticks. I even put a bunch of the yogurt raisins you like on top."

"Not hungry."

I hear a dish clatter. "I'll leave it here on your lab desk in case you want it later."

Might as well. There's plenty of room on my desk now.

"Mom and Dad took your computer away?"

No need to answer when the answer is obvious.

"A month isn't so long."

It is when you're an inventor. I shut my eyes. Isabelle has no idea what I am going through. My sister never breaks a rule.

Is she still here?

"What were you thinking, sneaking out to Beeson's Lake when you're grounded?"

Yep, still here. And I've already answered this question once today. Or tried to.

After my mother bandaged my leg and after she made me take a hot shower and after she made me eat a whole bowl of butternut squash soup, it was time to make me face my punishment. So this is what I did. I looked directly at my parents. I did not fidget, bob my eyebrows, or let my ears turn red. Nope. I stayed perfectly still. Then, in a calm, steady voice I said, "Mom and Dad, there's a dinosaur in Beeson's Lake."

★ TODAY'S MATH LESSON ★

4 new weeks of being grounded + 2 weeks I had left from my first grounding = 6 weeks.

0 computer + 0 video games + 0 TV + 0 phone calls + 0 fishing with Uncle Ant this summer = 0 life!

My father looked directly back at me and then, in a calm, steady voice he said, "Son, it's going to be a long time before you can prove it."

Isabelle is still jabbering away. ". . . and you could have fallen climbing out your window. And then diving into the deep, cold water after Joe? You both could have drowned. And for what? To find some stupid dinosaur? Have you completely lost your marbles?"

My eyelids fly open. What did she say? Joe sits up.

I sit up too. "What did you say?"

"I asked if you were crazy, which is dumb, I know, because clearly you are—"

"Before that. You said 'diving into the water after Joe.'"

"Uh . . . yeah. You did rescue the dog, didn't you?"

I am already leaping off the bed to sock-slide across my hardwood floor. I did rescue Joe. More importantly, I dove into DEEP WATER to do it. "Yeah!" I shout, doing a spin. "I did dive. I really, really did!"

TOP SECRET!
SCAB'S PERSONAL 411
★ SCAB'S FEARS ★

FEAR	WHY?
~~Deep water~~	~~I can't touch bottom!~~
Enchiladas	I don't trust food that's folded. (Who knows what it's hiding?)
Automatic sliding doors	Squish-o-matic your kid at the Food Mart! Have a nice day. ☺
The letter G	I can't write it in cursive. My teacher, Miss Sweetandsour, says my G's are saggy. So are her ears.
Ferns	Freaky branches? Curly tendrils? Spores?? Hello, alien species!
Getting lost	I'd miss my dog, Joe; my friends; and my family (even Tattletale Isabelle).

"Woof!" Joe thinks we are playing. He is chasing my foot.

"O-kay." She is watching me. "You're acting like it's the first time you've ever . . ."

"Another miracle," I shout when she doesn't finish. "Isabelle McNally shuts up." I collapse into a pile of clean clothes that I am supposed to fold but never do. I think this is the clean pile. Joe starts tugging on the end of my sock. I pull. He pulls. I pull.

"Owwww!" I cry out, half-laughing when I feel a tooth sink into my toe.

My sister gasps. "That's it!"

I fling a pair of my underwear at her. "What's it?"

Isabelle ducks and my underwear lands on my model B-52. "I get it now."

"What are you blabbering about now?"

"That's why you made the trick toe. And why you didn't want to do a kneeling dive last week. You were scared to dive."

I give her a ripper snort and get my foot back from Joe.

She comes closer. "And you're scared of the deep end, too, aren't you?"

"No," I say, but start folding my clothes, which is a dead giveaway.

"It's all right if you are—were—whatever."

"I'm not—wasn't." I roll a pair of socks up in a ball and throw it at her. She ducks. It hits my mom's cookbook, which falls over onto Abalard's paw.

The cat coughs up a furball. "*Eeeee-yaaaaaak.*"

"You could have told me," Isabelle says. "I would have understood."

"You would have tattled."

She doesn't say anything. Isabelle knows I am right. She picks up Joe's squeaky hot dog and tosses it into the hall for him. "At least you'll have a good story to tell Ashlynn and the class. I promise I'll let you tell it—"

"It's all yours. I'm not going back to class."

"You're quitting?"

"Yep."

"But why? If you're not scared anymore—"

"No reason to go now," I say, and break the news to her that our parents have canceled my fishing trip with Uncle Ant.

"But you can't quit now. What will I . . . ?"

"What?"

She shakes her head. "Never mind. Sorry about the trip. It's still two months away. Maybe they will change their minds."

"Maybe," I say, but we both know they won't. Once you get a punishment in our house, it's stuck to you like duct tape.

Joe brings his toy to me and drops it. I fling the hot dog into the closet. He races after it, his paws going every which way on the hardwood floor as he scrambles around the corner of the bed. I smile. I am feeling better. I heard my dad say something about getting Mexican takeout for dinner. I usually get spicy rice and beans, but tonight I might try something different. Maybe a taco. Or even an enchilada. After all, if I can swim the Deep End, maybe I can do one or two other things on my list too. We'll see.

My stomach gurgles. I slide across the floor to my desk. I do a spin. "Hey, Isabelle, do you want a peanut butter celery—?"

But she is gone.

13

Bravest Kid in the Universe

I am chugging pineapple-orange juice straight from the carton when, out of the corner of my eye, I spot a group of well-dressed rodents on a yellow background. My squirrel swim trunks are swinging in the air.

"Forget it, Isabelle," I say. "I'm not going."

My mom's head pops around the corner. She is smiling. Her smile disappears. "What is the rule, Scab?"

"Use a glass," I mutter. It's so much faster this way. Besides, it's not like I have fleas or the chicken pox or anything. Still, I get the glass.

"I'm driving Isabelle and Doyle to swimming today," says my mother. "Why don't you come too? It might be fun."

"I don't think so."

"I'd love to see you swim across the deep end."

I slam my palm into my forehead. Isabelle cannot keep her whale mouth shut for three seconds!

★ WEIRD STUFF YOUR PARENTS SAY ★

WHAT MY MOM SAYS	WHAT I SAY
What's the rule?	Don't you know?
Don't make me come up there.	Who's making you?
Is that the best excuse you've got?	Give me a minute and I'll come up with something better.
If all your friends jumped off a cliff, would you jump too?	Uh, no. That would hurt.
I hope one day you have a kid just like you.	Thanks!

"No, thanks." I start gulping juice and don't stop until it's all gone.

"If you won't do it for you and you won't do it for me, how about for your sister?"

"Isabelle?" Her name echoes off the bottom of my empty glass. "What's she got to do with it?"

"I'm not supposed to tell you this, but—"

"What?"

My mother leans in. "Isabelle would only take the Salmon class if you took it too."

This doesn't sound like my I-am-better-than-you-at-everything sister. "Why?" I ask.

"Maybe she was a little scared about what to expect. Maybe it made her feel better to have her brother there too."

Isabelle scared? Hardly. Wanted me there? Never.

I think about it. Well. Maybe.

The front doorbell rings.

"That's probably Doyle," says my mom.

I follow her into the hall. When she opens the door, my best friend is leaning against the door frame, gulping air. His cheeks are red. "You're not gonna believe . . . your pictures, Scab . . . it was something there . . . and they think . . . a diver . . . and they're bringing it up."

"Doyle, relax," says my mother. "Scab, what's he talking about it?"

"I don't know."

"I do," says a voice behind us. Isabelle is standing on the stairs. "He's talking about the digital photos that Scab's submersible took at Beeson's Lake."

I shake my head. "No, he's not. Mom and Dad took my computer away. I never got to see—"

"You didn't," she says, wincing. "But I did. Sorry, Mom. I was just so curious. Besides, I never expected to see anything. I mean, a dinosaur in Beeson's Lake? Come on. But then, when I was looking through the pictures, I saw—"

"Zenobia!" I cry. "You saw the dinosaur!"

"No-ooo. But I did see something, some kind of object. I made a CD and gave it—"

"She gave it to me." Doyle jumps in, his voice at full strength again. "I showed it to my dad, who showed it to Mrs. Scudder at the public library, who showed it to Miss Waddington at the historical society." He pulls out a piece of paper from his back pocket, unfolds it, and hands it to my mom. "Here's a copy of the newspaper article Miss Waddington found.

See, back in the 1940s, a couple of guys robbed the Granite First National Bank. They got away with a bunch of cash and gold bars."

"Are you saying—?"

"We didn't find a dinosaur in Beeson's Lake, Scab. We found a 1940 Buick." My best friend's eyes are huge. "And it's probably full of gold! That's what I've been trying to tell you. They're bringing the car up out of the water right now!"

"Let's go," says my mother.

"What about swimming lessons?"

"You'll be a little late, Isabelle."

I snatch the squirrel trunks off my mom's arm and race up the stairs. "Wait for me. I have to get a towel." And Joe. "Joe!" I shout.

"You're coming?" asks Isabelle.

"I'm coming." I punch her in the shoulder. But not that hard.

She smiles and punches me back. But not that hard.

In the car, Doyle and I are bouncing all over the place. "Mom, go faster."

"I'm not running a red light, Scab."

"They'll probably give us some gold as a reward," I say.

"We'll be rich," says Doyle, who is between Isabelle and me.

"I doubt it," says Isabelle.

"They'll probably put our picture in the newspaper," I say. Sitting behind us, Joe licks the back of my neck. "Yours too." I laugh.

"We'll be famous," says Doyle.

"I doubt it," says Isabelle.

"Be sure to tell the reporter everything, Scab," says Doyle. "You know, about how you first wrestled with Zenobia and broke your fishing pole, how you invented the Surveillance Submersible, and how you went in the water to rescue Joe. Maybe I should tell it. You might leave something out. I'll give 'em the headline, too—'*Bravest Kid in the Universe.*'"

Sweet!

We knock knuckles.

I look past him at Isabelle. She looks at me. And for once, my sister doesn't say a thing.

I don't even have to fart.

We both know I'm not that brave. Maybe someday I might be. When there are no more automatic doors or alien ferns or cursive G's in the world. When I know I will never lose my family. Maybe then I'll be the bravest kid alive.

Then again, I have a feeling there will always be something on my top secret list of fears.

But you dive in anyway, right?

SCAB'S ADVENTURES

CONTINUE

Secrets of a Lab Rat

SCAB FOR ~~PRESIDENT~~
~~VICE-PRESIDENT~~
~~SECRETARY~~
TREASURER?

COMING SPRING 2011

Missy Malone is an Alien . . . Pass it On

Scab, please remove the number two pencil from your nose," says Miss Sweetandsour. "You know what to do."

I know what to do, all right. I just don't want to do it.

I am supposed to stand up, which is dumb because in two seconds I will have to sit right back down again. Miss Sweeten is giving me that squished up lemon face—the one that earned her the nickname Miss Sweetandsour. I have no choice but to obey my teacher. I blow the pencil out of my left nostril. There's a wet glob of tan snot on the eraser. I get to my feet. I stand to the left of my desk and try not to look at Missy Malone, who is standing to the right of my desk. I snap my wrist to zing the snot chunk in her direction. Too gooey. Won't budge.

Every Friday our teacher makes us play Fly Around the World. It's a math flash card game. Miss Sweetandsour goes through a stack of addition, subtraction, multiplication, and division flash cards. She flips one up for the champion and the challenger to do in their heads. Whichever kid shouts out the right answer first gets to be the champion and 'fly on' to the next challenger. The idea is to see how many kids you can beat as you move around the classroom.

I hate the game. Not because I don't like math (I do), but because I never win. That's the problem. Nobody ever wins, except Missy Malone. She flies around the world, yelling out the answers before her challengers even finish reading the cards. It's no wonder my friends and I call her Never Missy. She sits in front of me so I am usually her first victim. Never Missy has already beaten me once today and is back to whip my butt again. For her, the game is Fly Around the World. For the rest of us, it is Crash and Burn.

Never Missy smells like burned onion rings. She stares at me through brown bangs so shiny they look wet. She smirks. Two little dimples appear on each side of her mouth. Easy target, she is thinking. She is right. I hate that she is right.

My hands are sweaty. So are my armpits. The meatballs I had for lunch are wrestling in my stomach. Miss Sweetandsour is shuffling her flash cards.

Leaning back, I look for my best friend. Doyle Ferguson is in the far front corner by the cubby rack. We're so far apart he might as well be in Antarctica. When I see him, I cross my eyes, scrunch my nose, and point to Never Missy's back. Doyle pulls his mouth all the way back with both thumbs. He sticks his tongue out and waggles it. We both think Never Missy is a space alien—and not in a good way, either. Her mustard-onion-chili breath can peel the paint off your bike. She wears tiny paper party-favor umbrellas in her hair. She never takes off her puffy, purple jacket. *Never.* We think it's because Never Missy doesn't want anybody to see the slimy green tentacles she's got hiding under there.

"Scab? Missy?" Miss Sweetandsour is ready.

I wipe my sticky hands on the sides of my jeans. This is it. This time I am going to beat Never Missy. I know, I know, I say it every Friday afternoon, but today I mean it.